HAVE YOU READ THESE
NARWHAL AND JELLY BOOKS?

NARWHAL: UNICORN OF THE SEA!

PEANUT BUTTER AND JELLY

SUPER NARWHAL AND JELLY JOLT

BEN CLANTON

tundra

FOR THEO!
MY SUPER SON!

Text and illustrations copyright © 2017 by Ben Clanton

Tundra Books, an imprint of Penguin Random House Canada Young Readers, a Penguin Random House Company

Library and Archives Canada Cataloguing in Publication

Clanton, Ben, 1988-, author, illustrator
Super Narwhal and Jelly Jolt / Ben Clanton.

(A Narwhal and Jelly book)
Issued in print and electronic formats.
ISBN 978-1-101-91829-6 (hardback).—ISBN 978-1-101-91830-2 (epub)

I. Graphic novels. I. Title.

PZ7.7.C53Sup 2017   j741.5'973   C2016-905226-5
                                                C2016-905227-3

Published simultaneously in the United States of America by Tundra Books of Northern New York, an imprint of Penguin Random House Canada Young Readers, a Penguin Random House Company

Library of Congress Control Number: 2016948348

Edited by Tara Walker and Jessica Burgess
Designed by Ben Clanton and Andrew Roberts
The super-duper artwork in this book was rendered in colored pencil, watercolor, ink and colored digitally.
The text was handlettered by Ben Clanton.

Photos: (waffle) © Tiger Images/Shutterstock; (strawberry) © Valentina Razumova/Shutterstock; (pickle) © dominitsky/Shutterstock; (tuba) Internet Archive Book Images

Printed and bound in China

www.penguinrandomhouse.ca

6 7 8 9   21 20 19 18

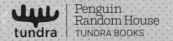

Penguin
Random House
tundra | TUNDRA BOOKS

CONTENTS

swoosh!

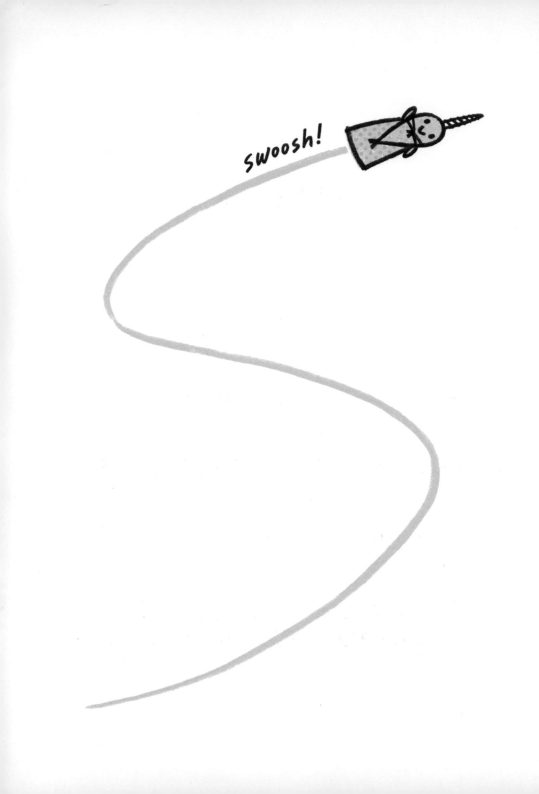

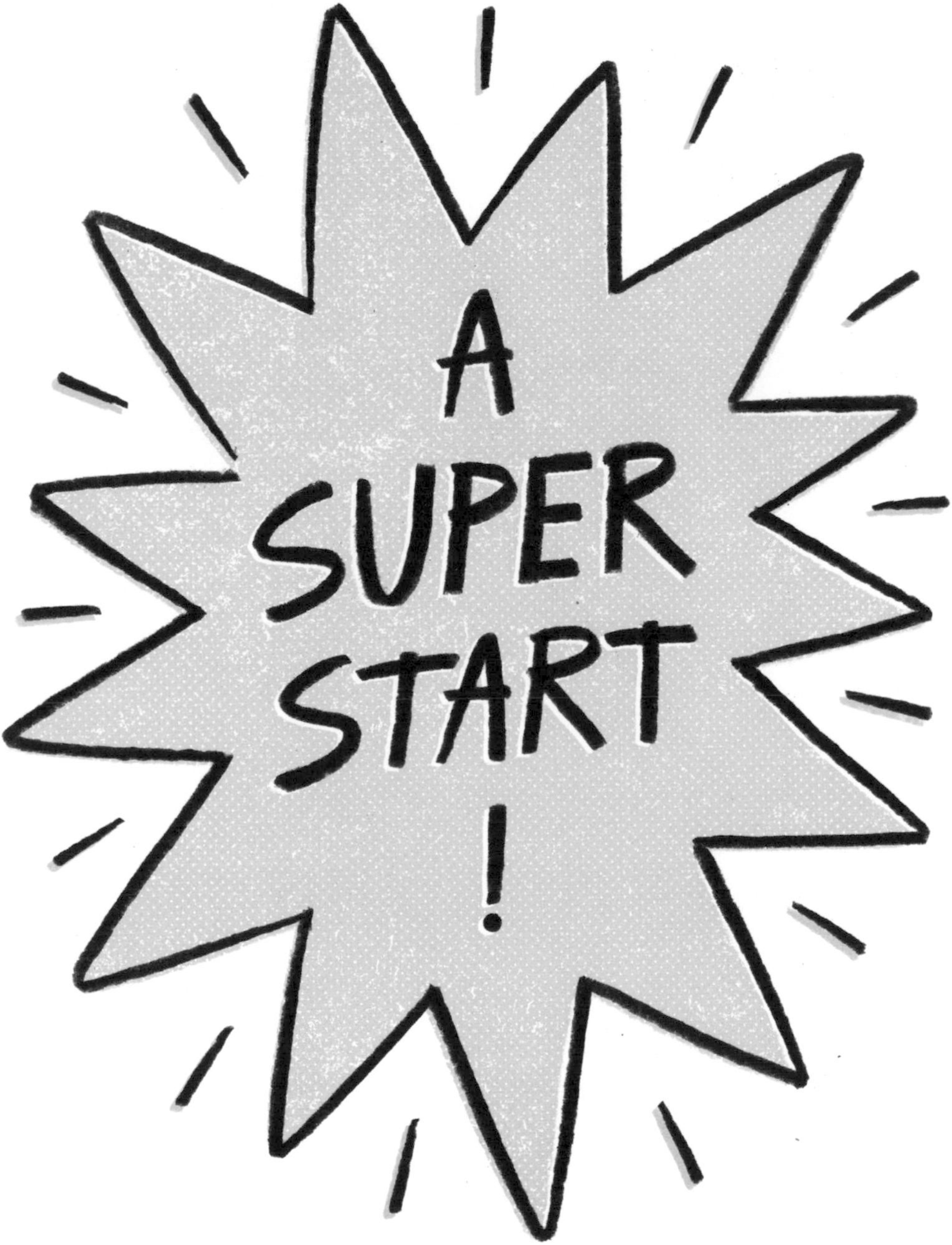
A SUPER START!

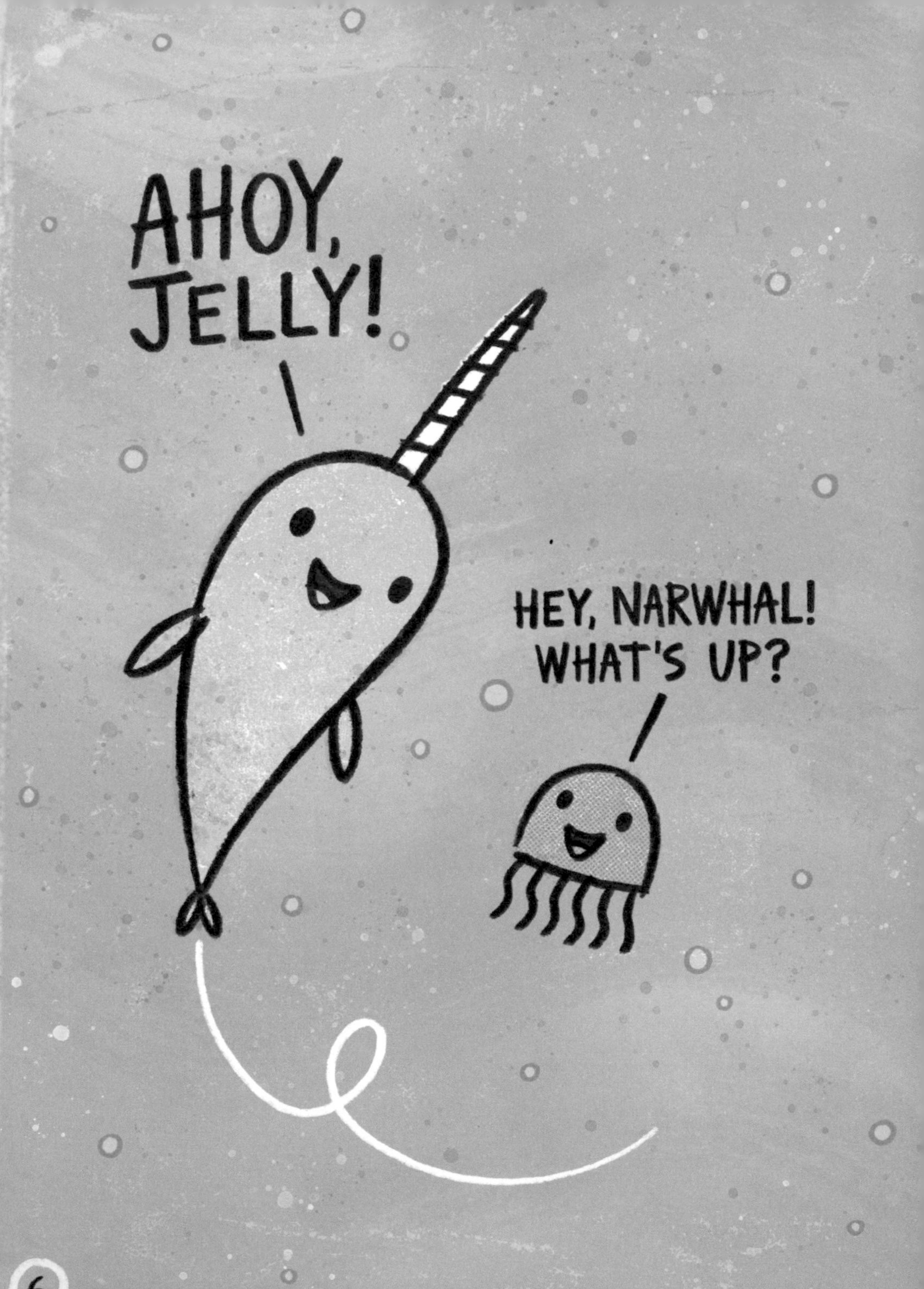
AHOY, JELLY!
HEY, NARWHAL! WHAT'S UP?

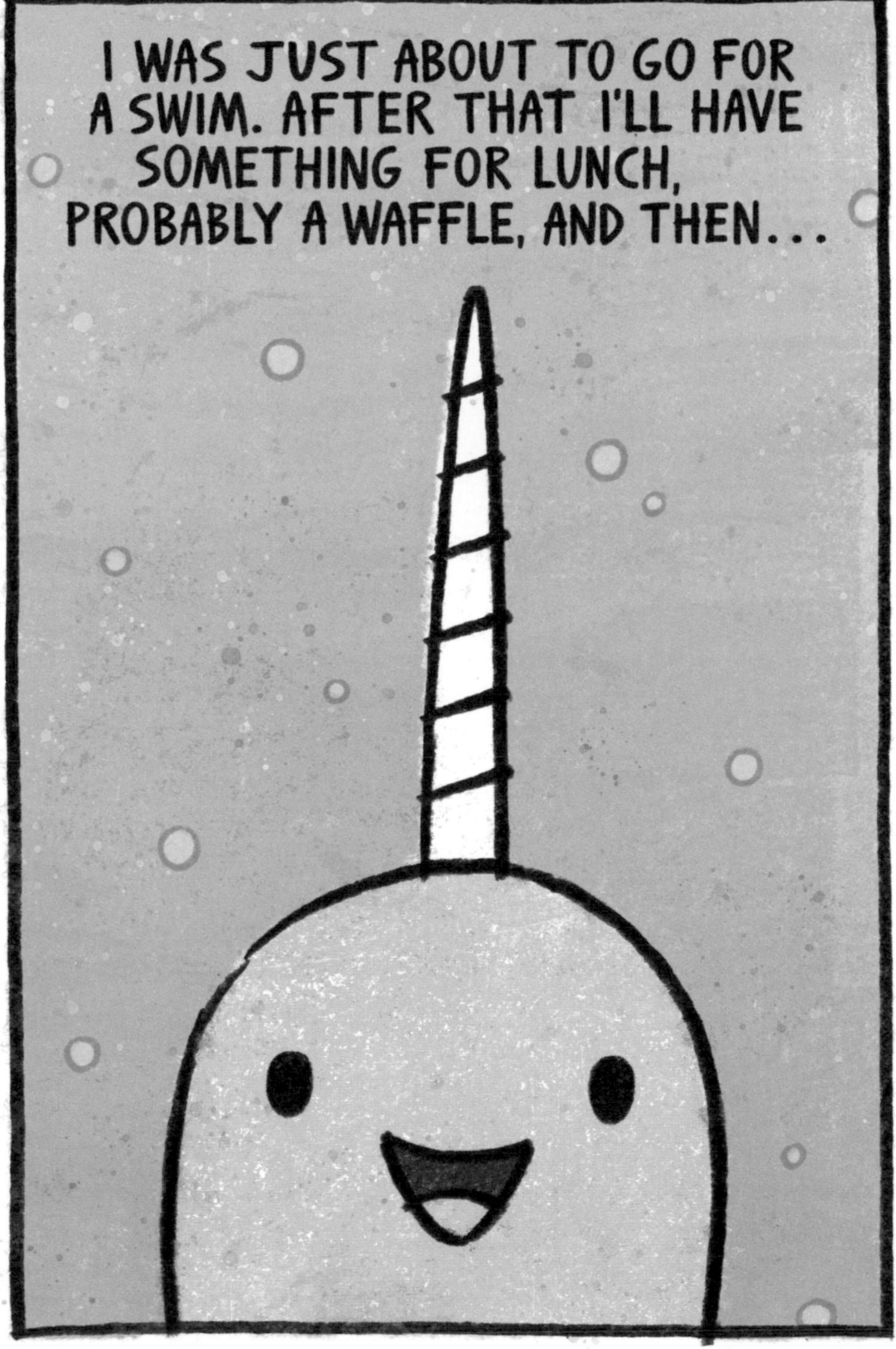
I WAS JUST ABOUT TO GO FOR A SWIM. AFTER THAT I'LL HAVE SOMETHING FOR LUNCH, PROBABLY A WAFFLE, AND THEN...

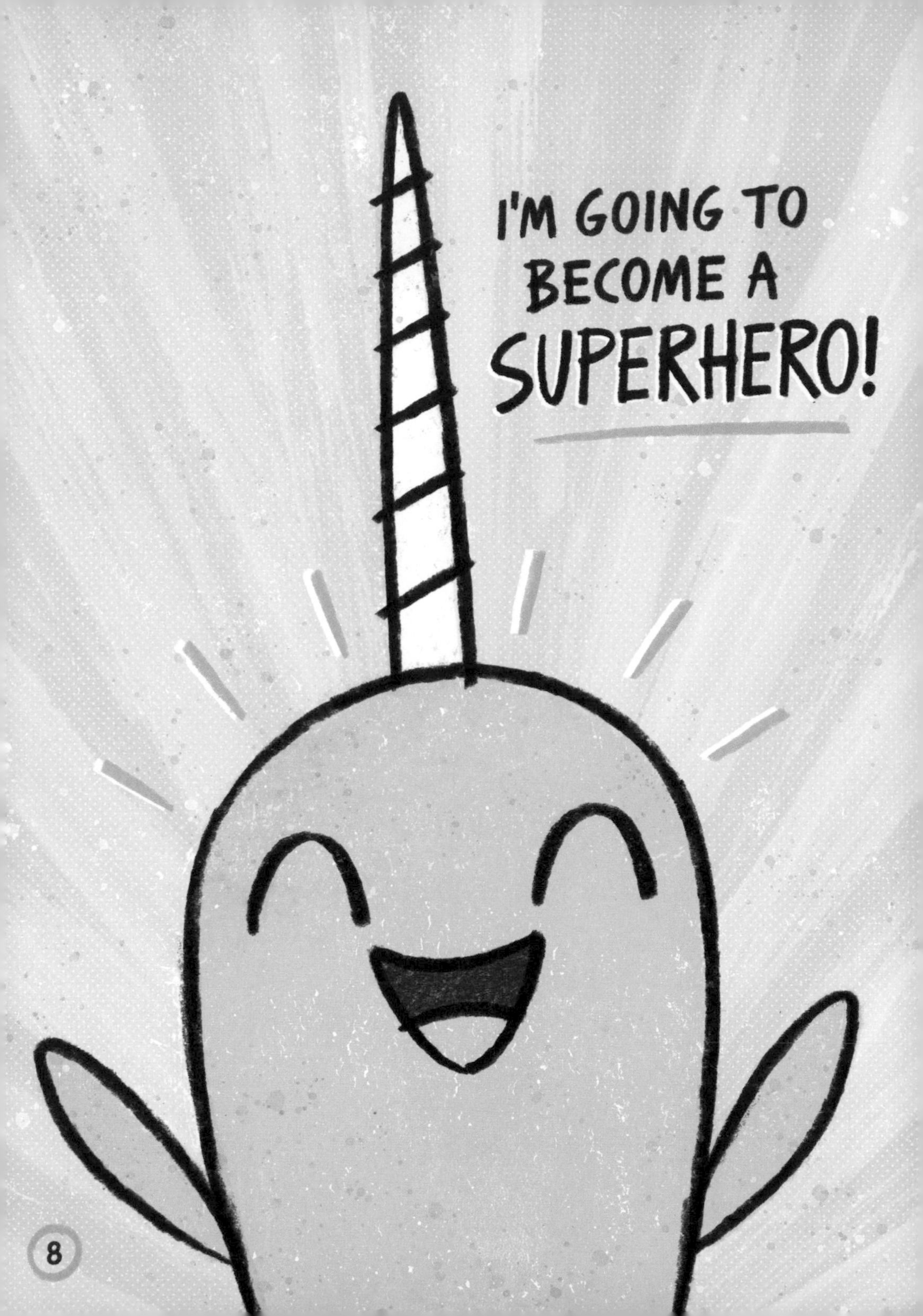
I'M GOING TO BECOME A SUPERHERO!

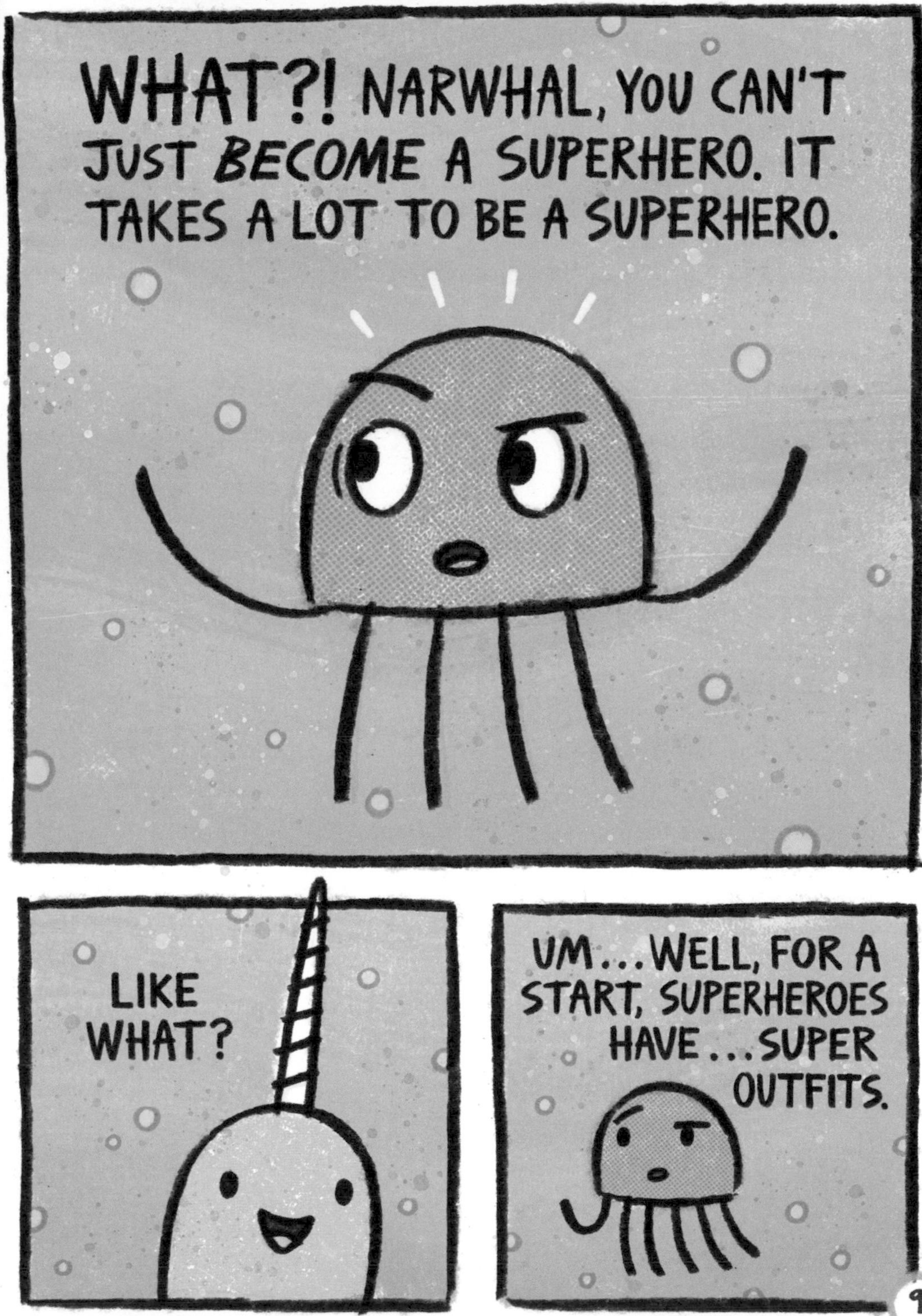
WHAT?! NARWHAL, YOU CAN'T JUST *BECOME* A SUPERHERO. IT TAKES A LOT TO BE A SUPERHERO.
LIKE WHAT?
UM... WELL, FOR A START, SUPERHEROES HAVE... SUPER OUTFITS.

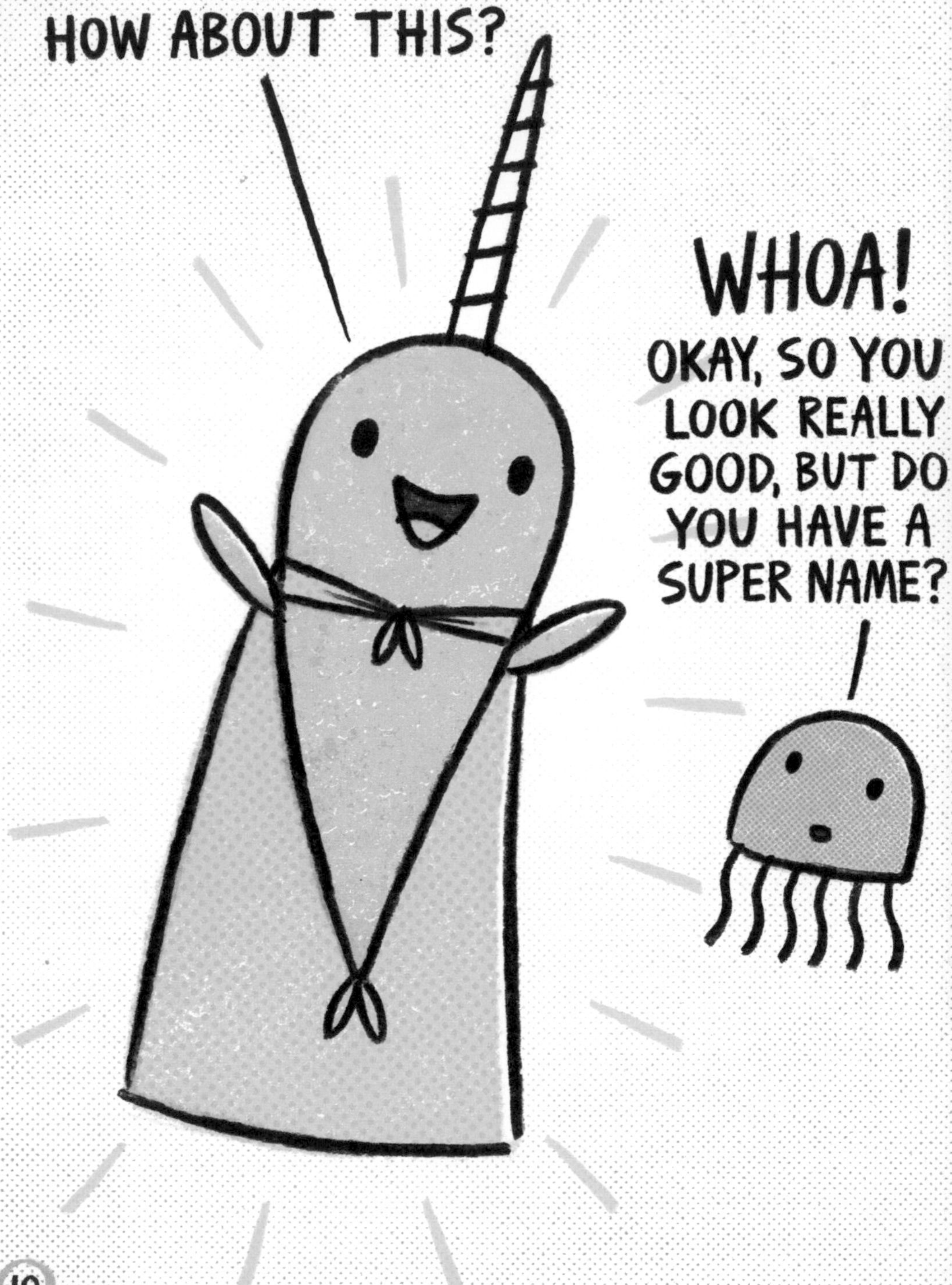
HOW ABOUT THIS?
WHOA!
OKAY, SO YOU LOOK REALLY GOOD, BUT DO YOU HAVE A SUPER NAME?

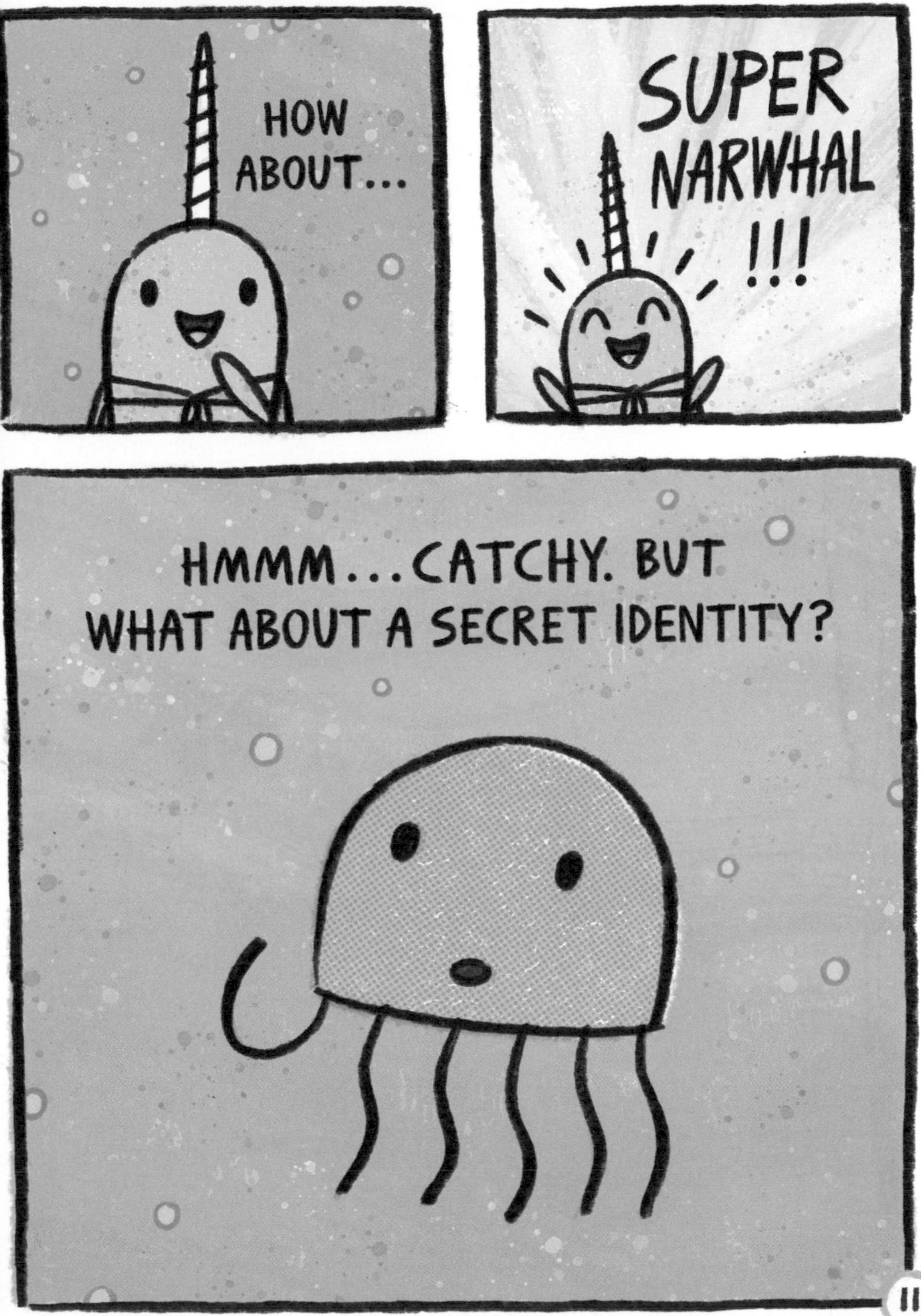
HOW ABOUT...
SUPER NARWHAL !!!
HMMM...CATCHY. BUT WHAT ABOUT A SECRET IDENTITY?

JELLY JOLT THE SUPER SIDEKICK!

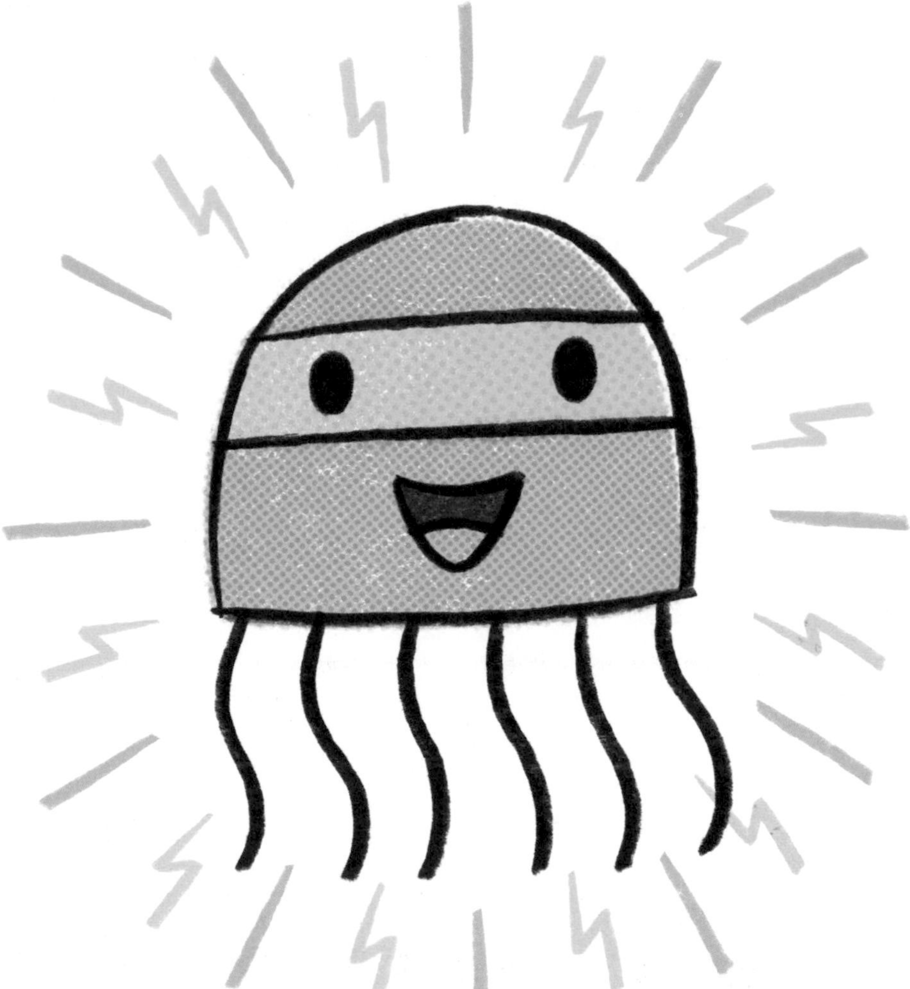

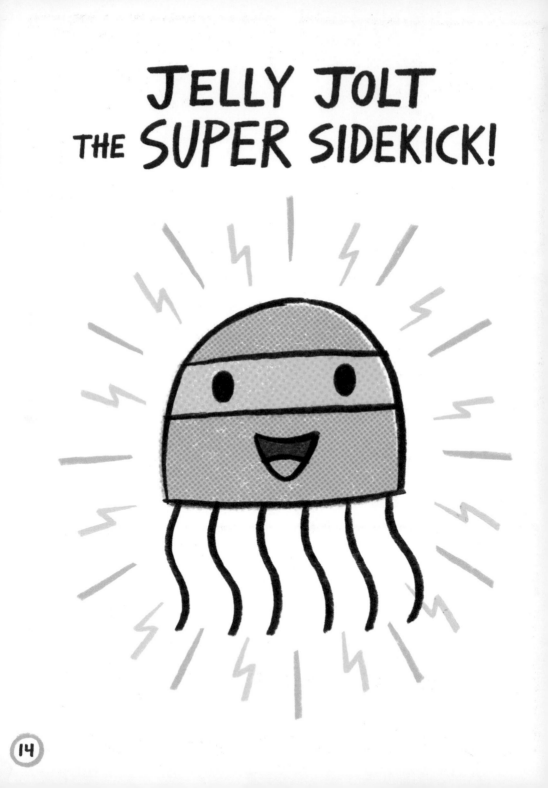

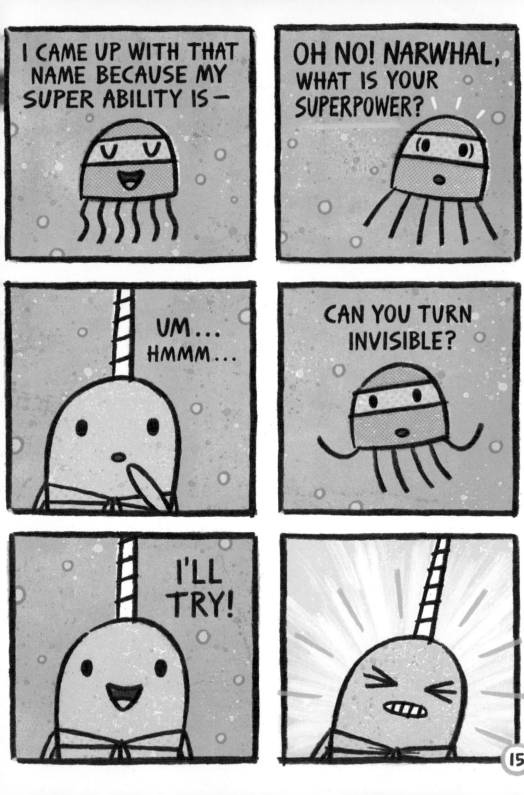

CAN YOU FLY? BREATHE FIRE?

ANYTHING?

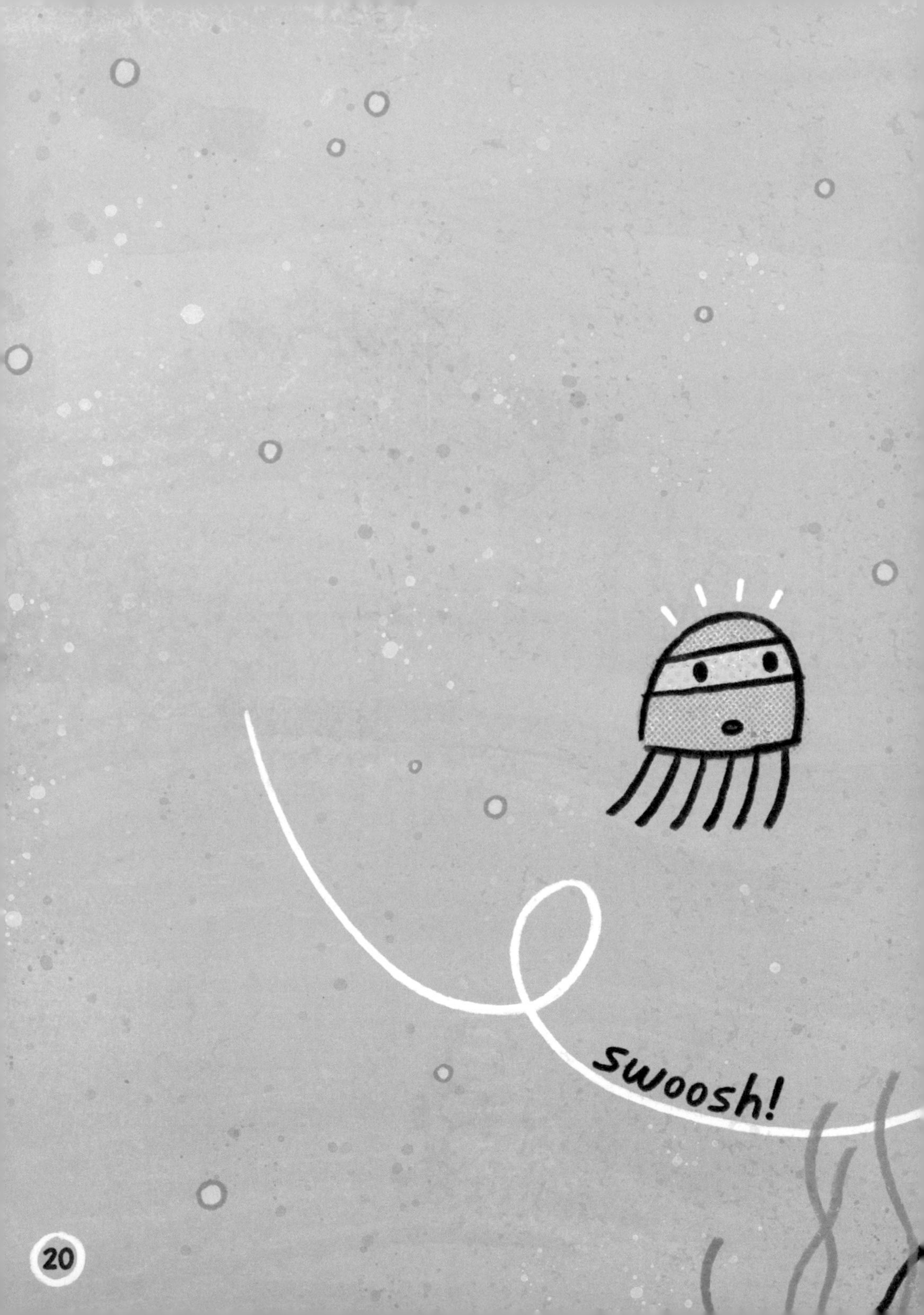
swoosh!

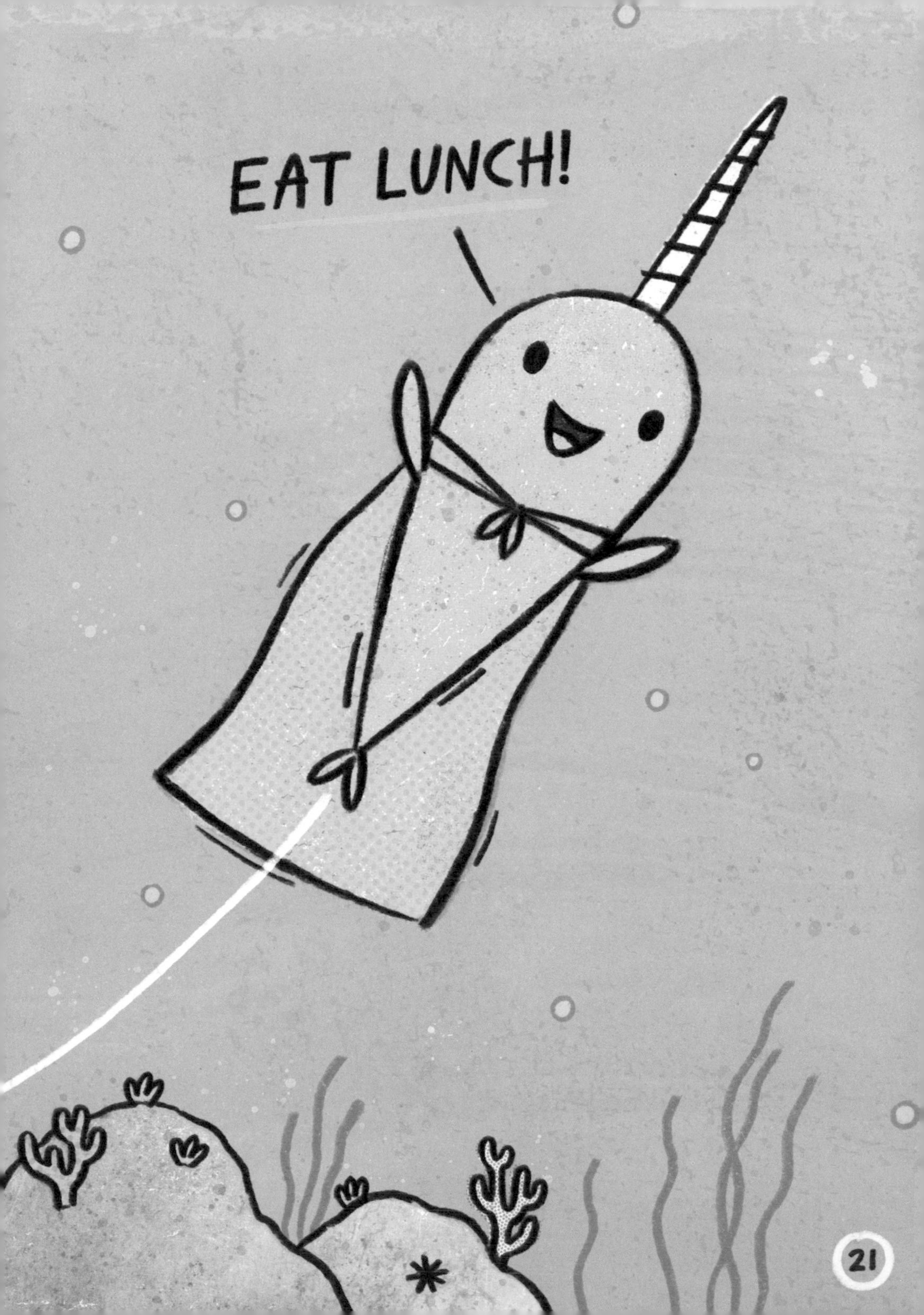
EAT LUNCH!

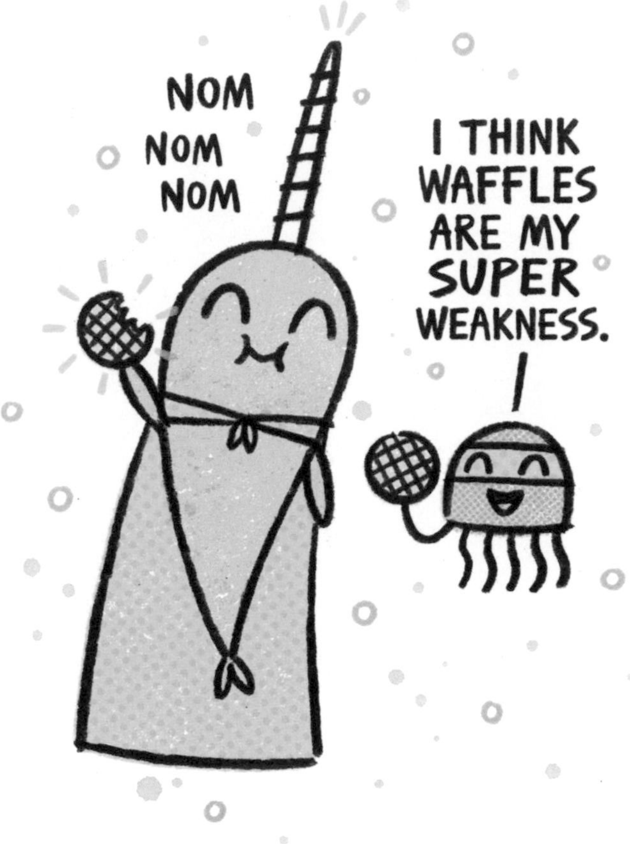
NOM
NOM
NOM
I THINK WAFFLES ARE MY SUPER WEAKNESS.

SUPER SEA CREATURES

REAL SEA CREATURES WITH REAL SUPER-AWESOME ABILITIES

THE MIMIC OCTOPUS CAN CHANGE ITS COLOR, SHAPE AND MOVEMENTS TO LOOK LIKE OTHER SEA LIFE SUCH AS SNAKES, LIONFISH, STINGRAYS AND JELLYFISH.

STOP COPYING ME!

STOP COPYING ME!

DOLPHINS SLEEP WITH ONLY HALF OF THEIR BRAIN AND WITH ONE EYE OPEN TO WATCH FOR THREATS.

DOLPHINS CAN ALSO "SEE" INSIDE MANY ANIMALS BY USING SOUND WAVES.

I SEE YOU HAD A WAFFLE FOR LUNCH!

NARWHAL, YOU'RE

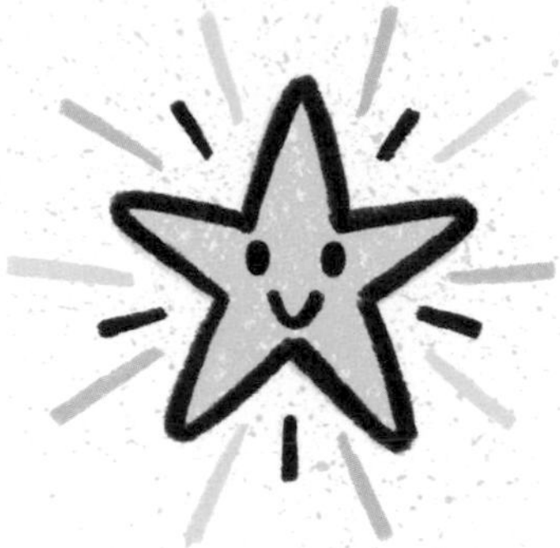

A SUPERSTAR!

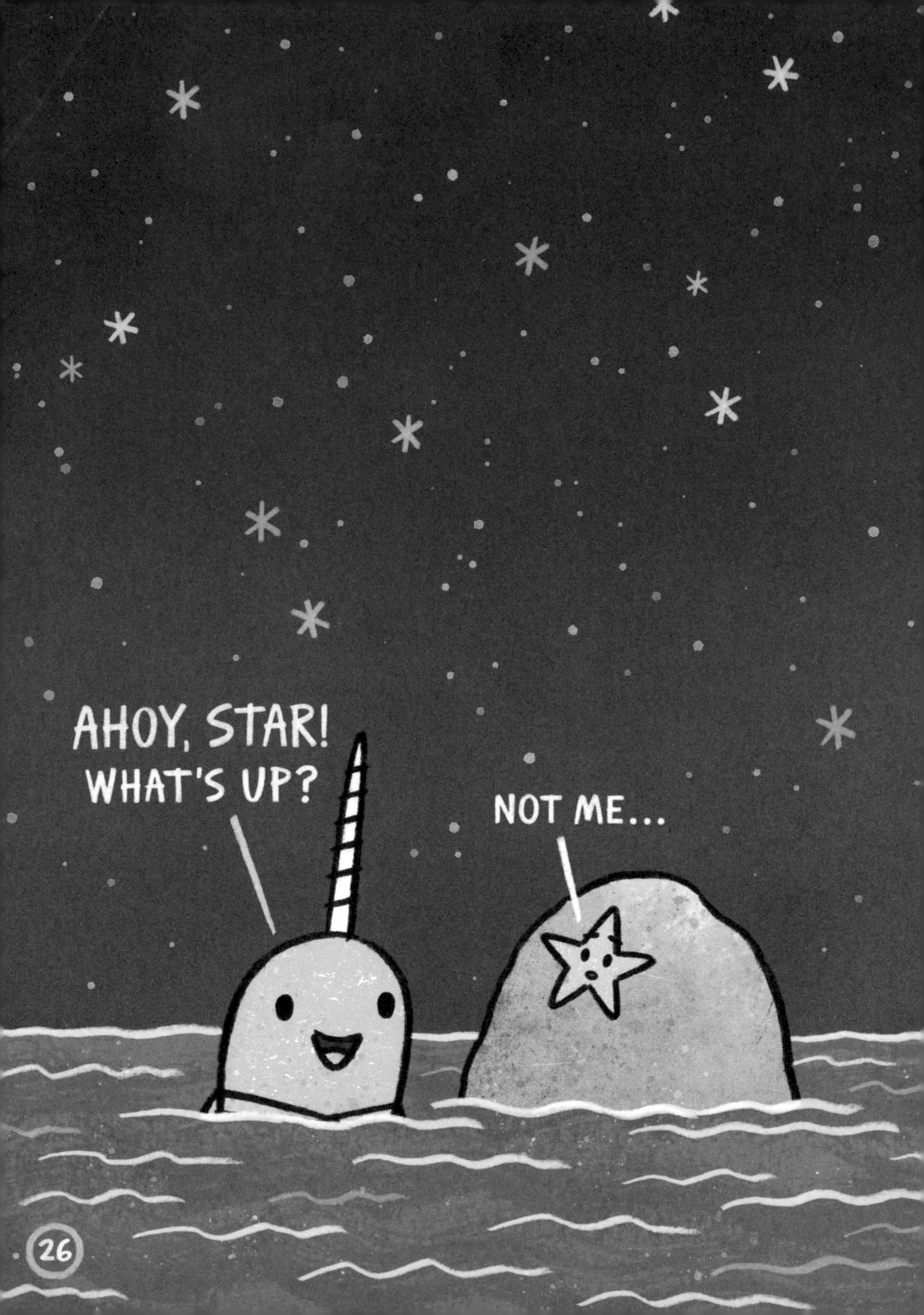
AHOY, STAR! WHAT'S UP?
NOT ME...

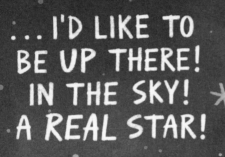

... I'D LIKE TO BE UP THERE! IN THE SKY! A REAL STAR!

SOUNDS STELLAR!

MAYBE I AM A REAL STAR, BUT I FELL TO EARTH AND HIT MY HEAD OR SOMETHING AND NOW I DON'T REMEMBER!

MAYBE! WANT ME TO TRY THROWING YOU UP THERE?

OKAY!

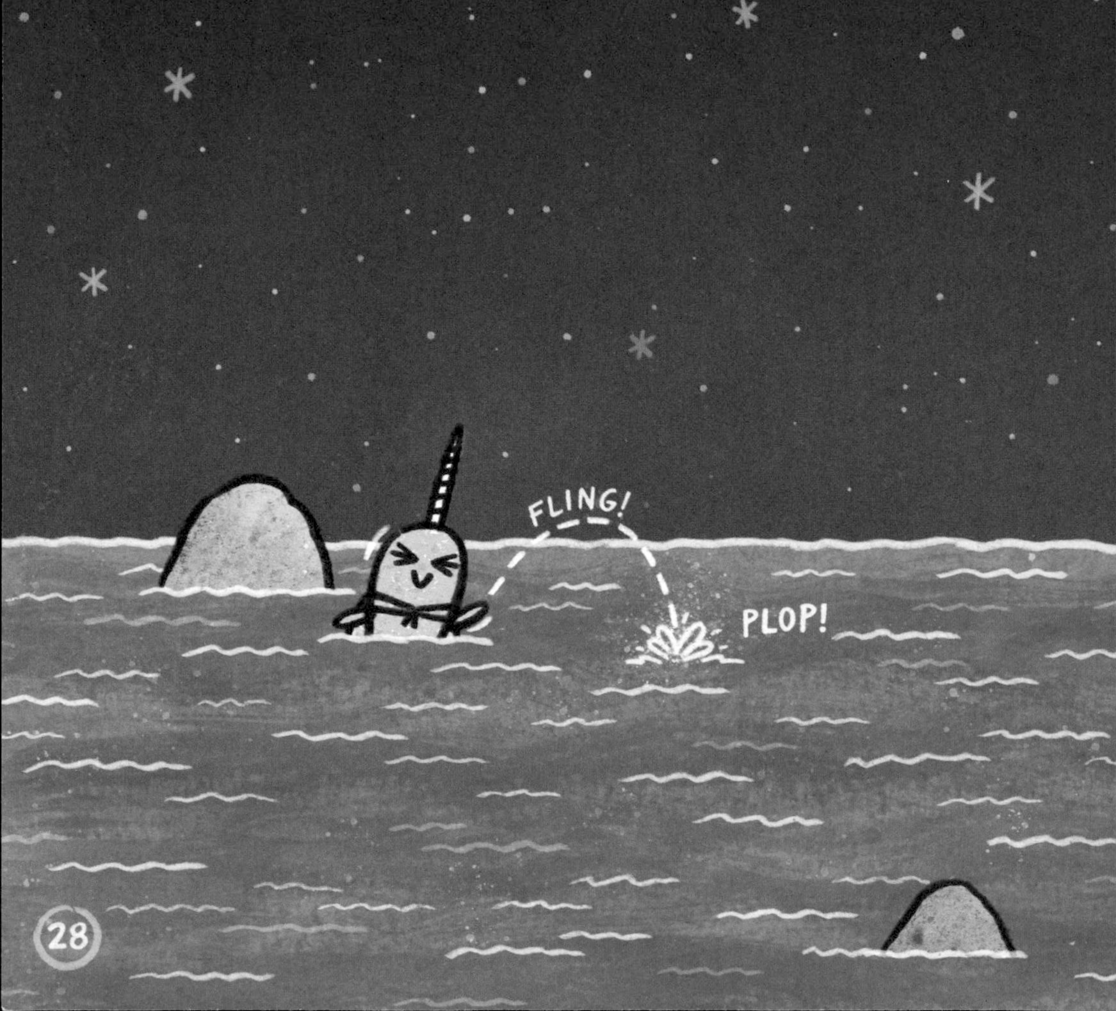
FLING!
PLOP!

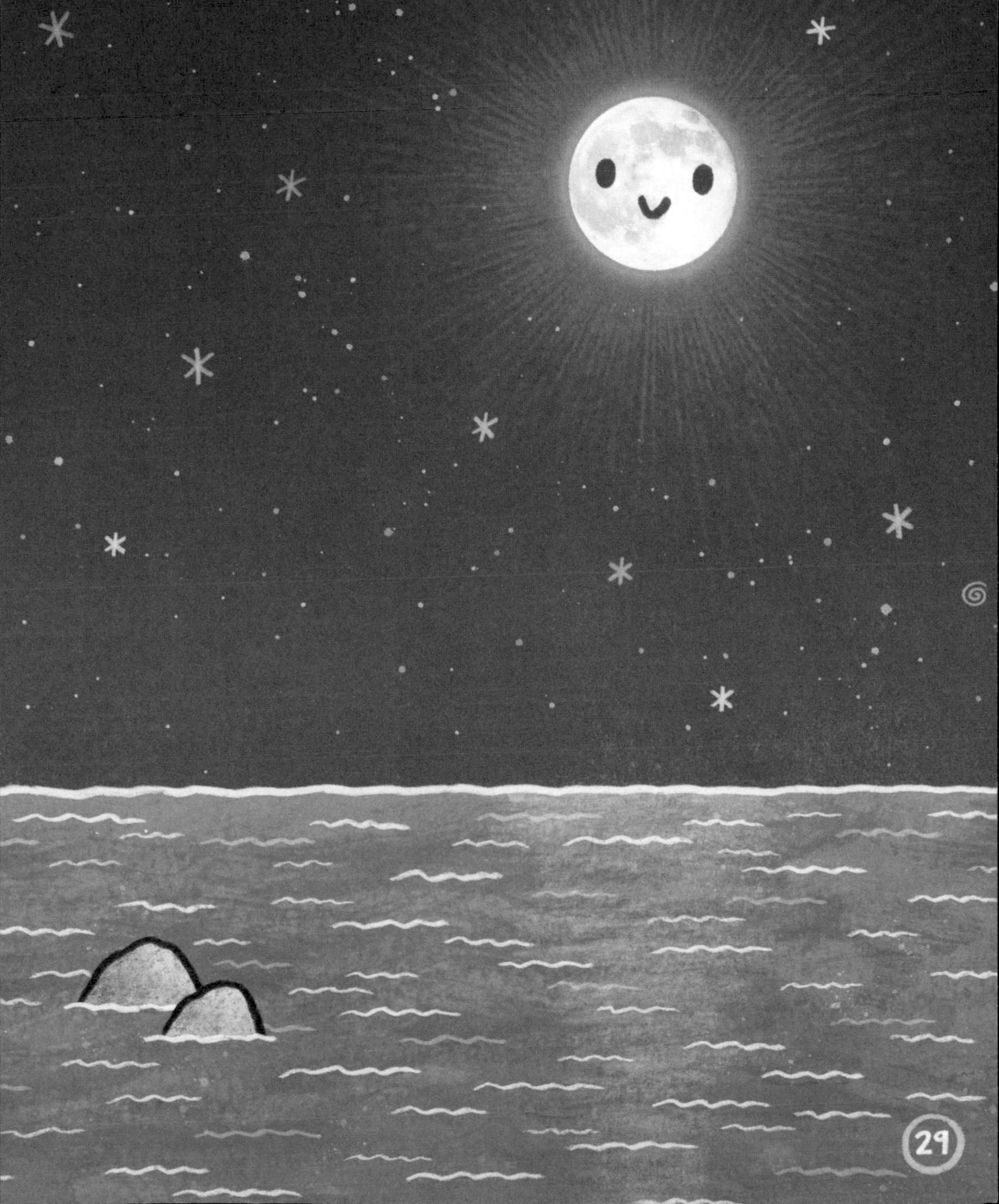

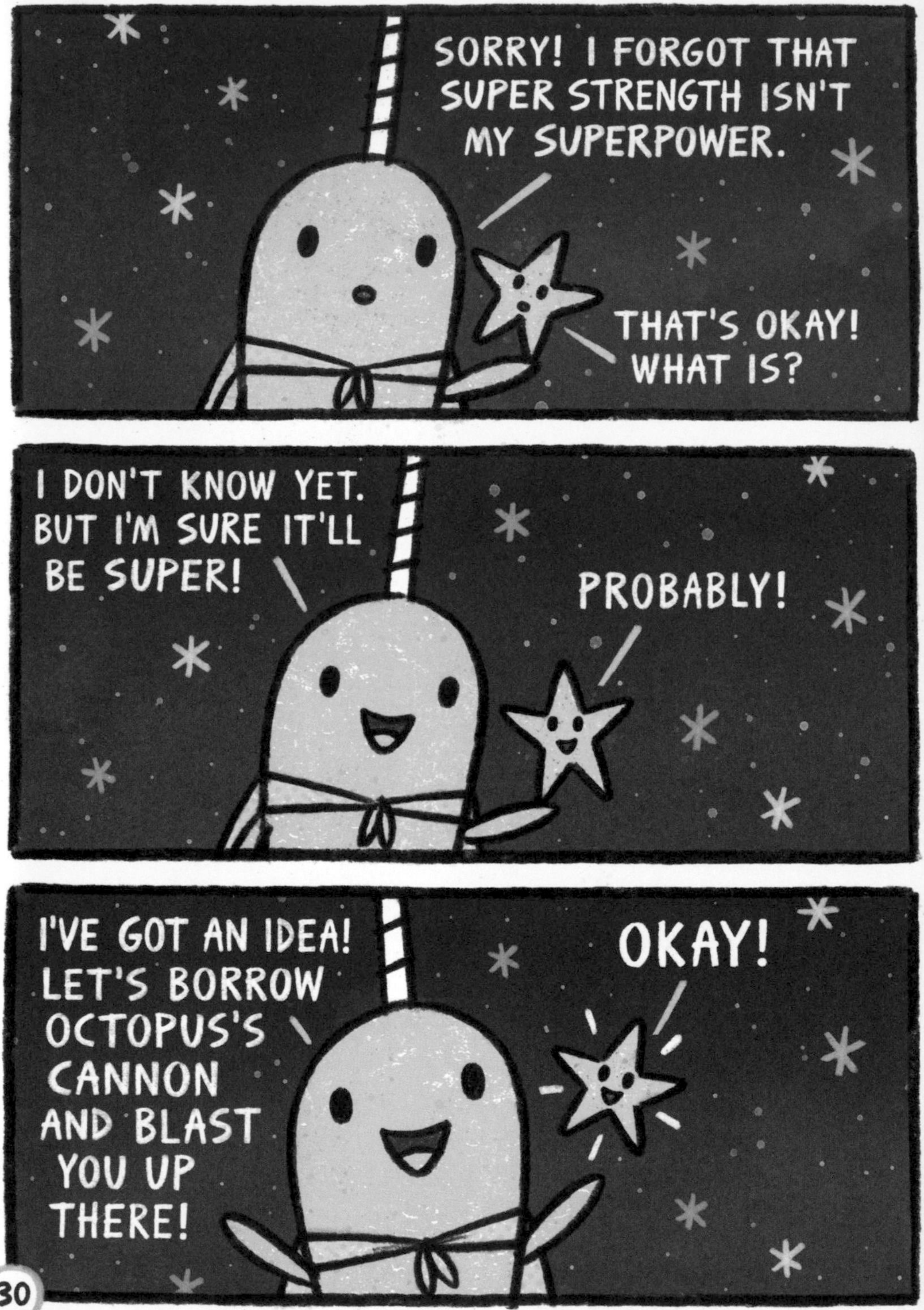
SORRY! I FORGOT THAT SUPER STRENGTH ISN'T MY SUPERPOWER.
THAT'S OKAY! WHAT IS?
I DON'T KNOW YET. BUT I'M SURE IT'LL BE SUPER!
PROBABLY!
I'VE GOT AN IDEA! LET'S BORROW OCTOPUS'S CANNON AND BLAST YOU UP THERE!
OKAY!

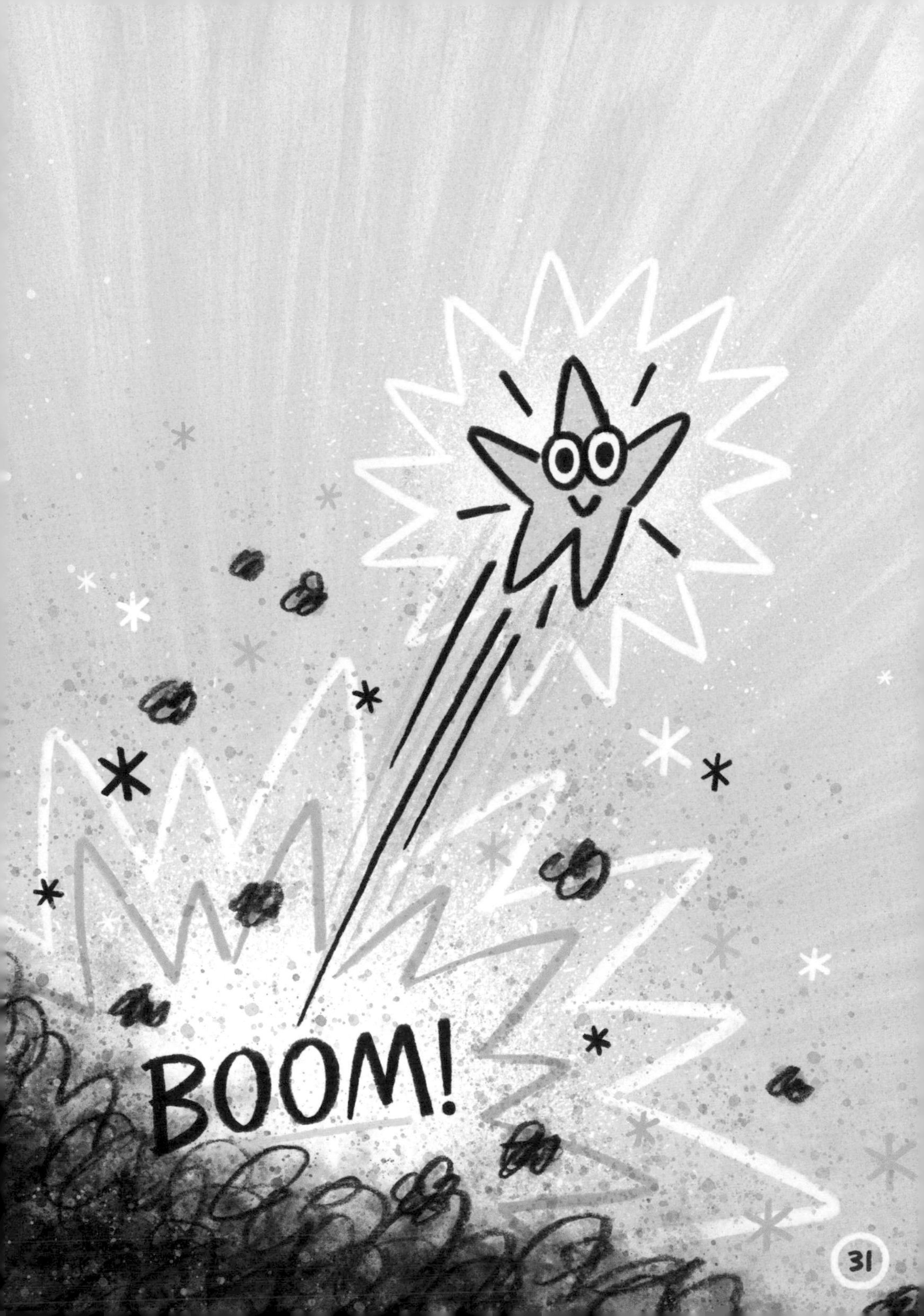
BOOM!

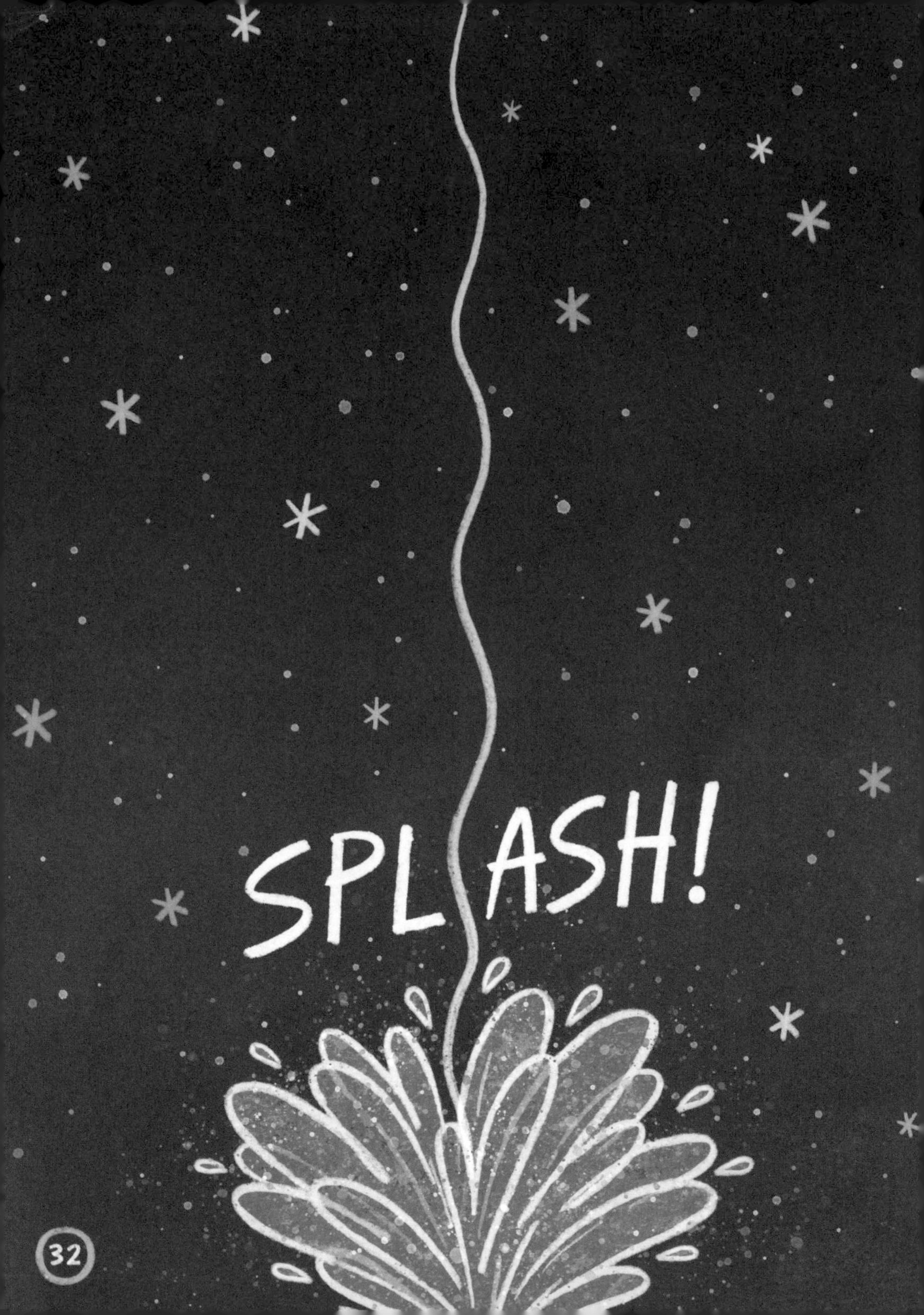
SPLASH!

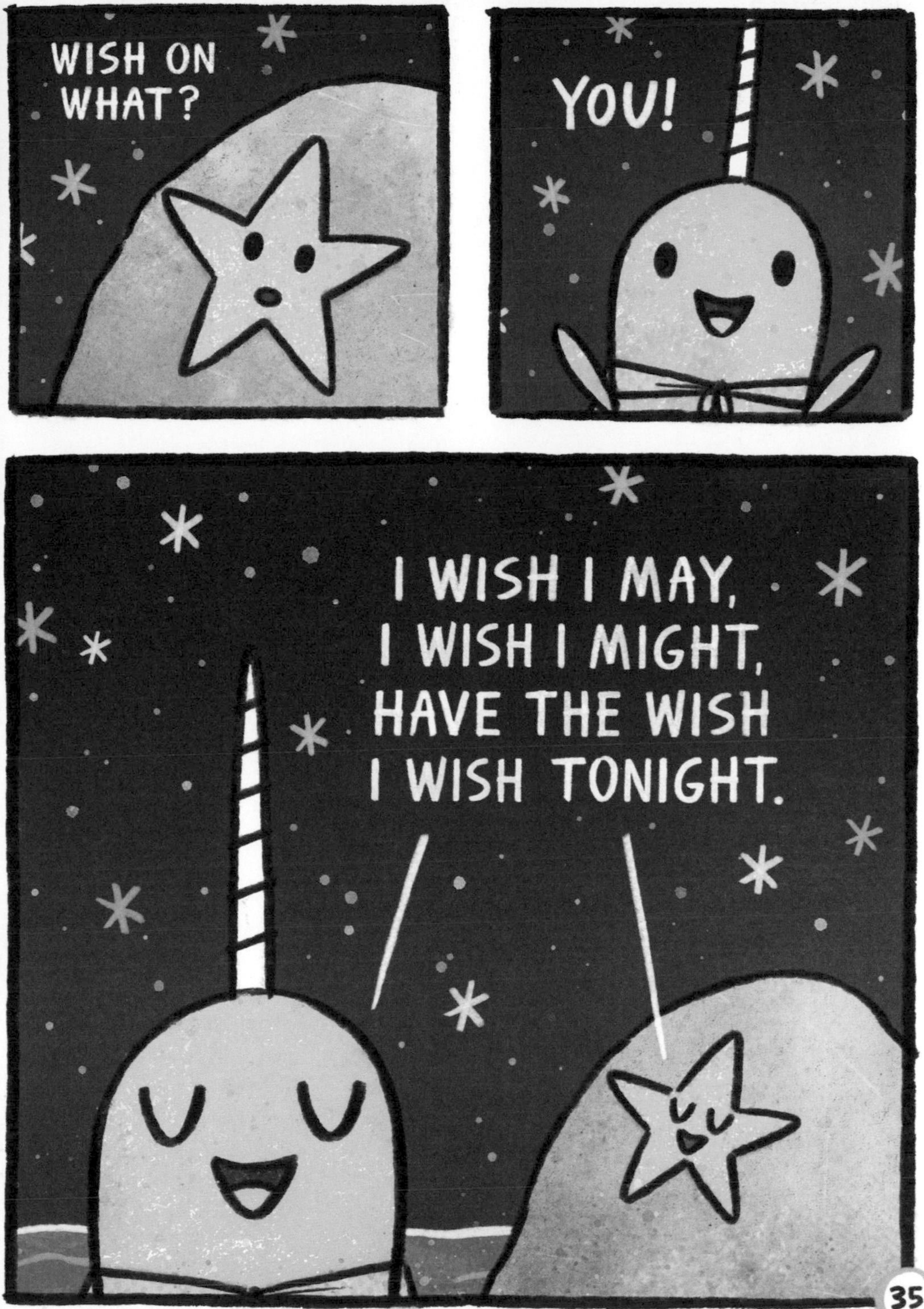
WISH ON WHAT?
YOU!
I WISH I MAY, I WISH I MIGHT, HAVE THE WISH I WISH TONIGHT.

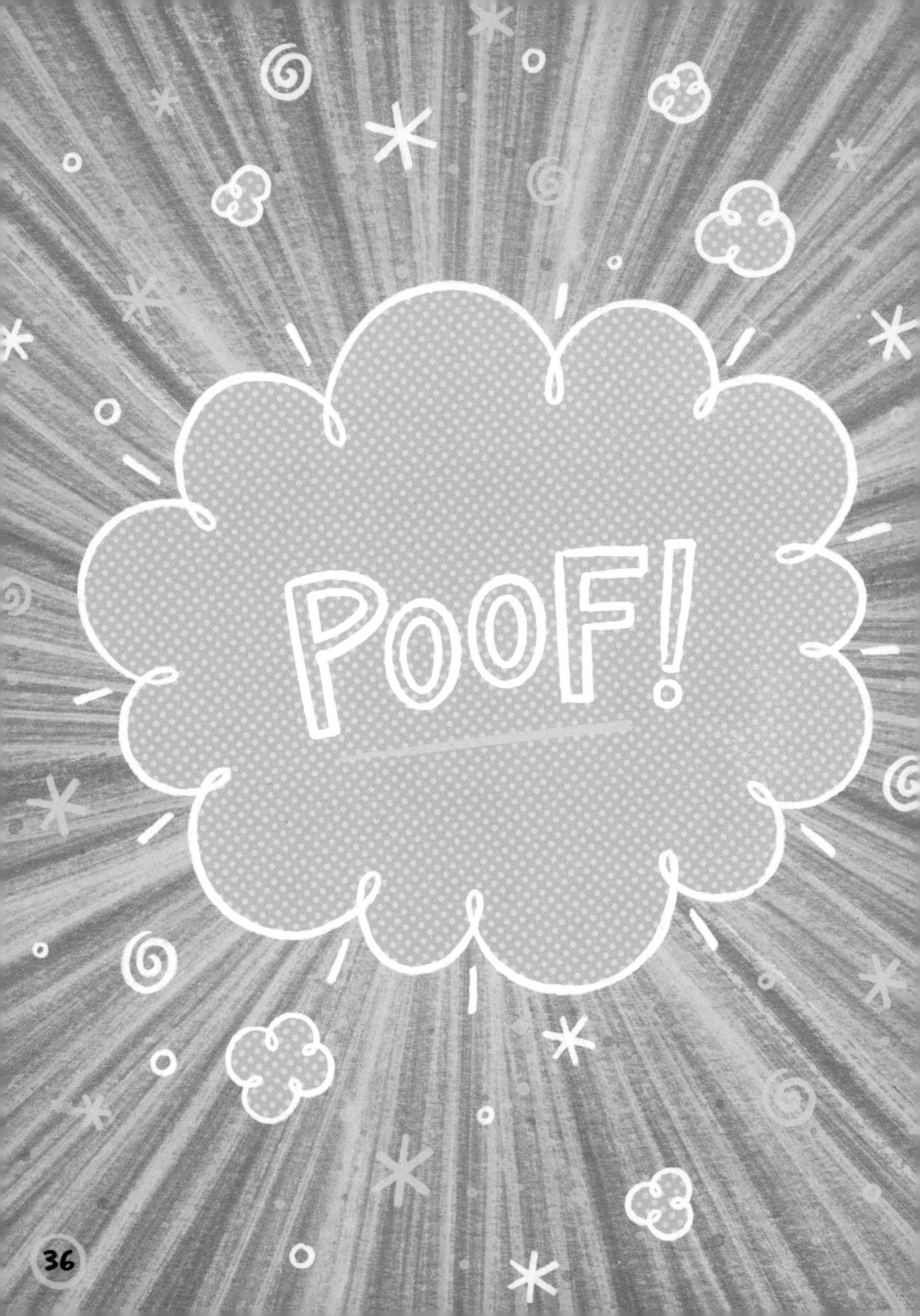
POOF!

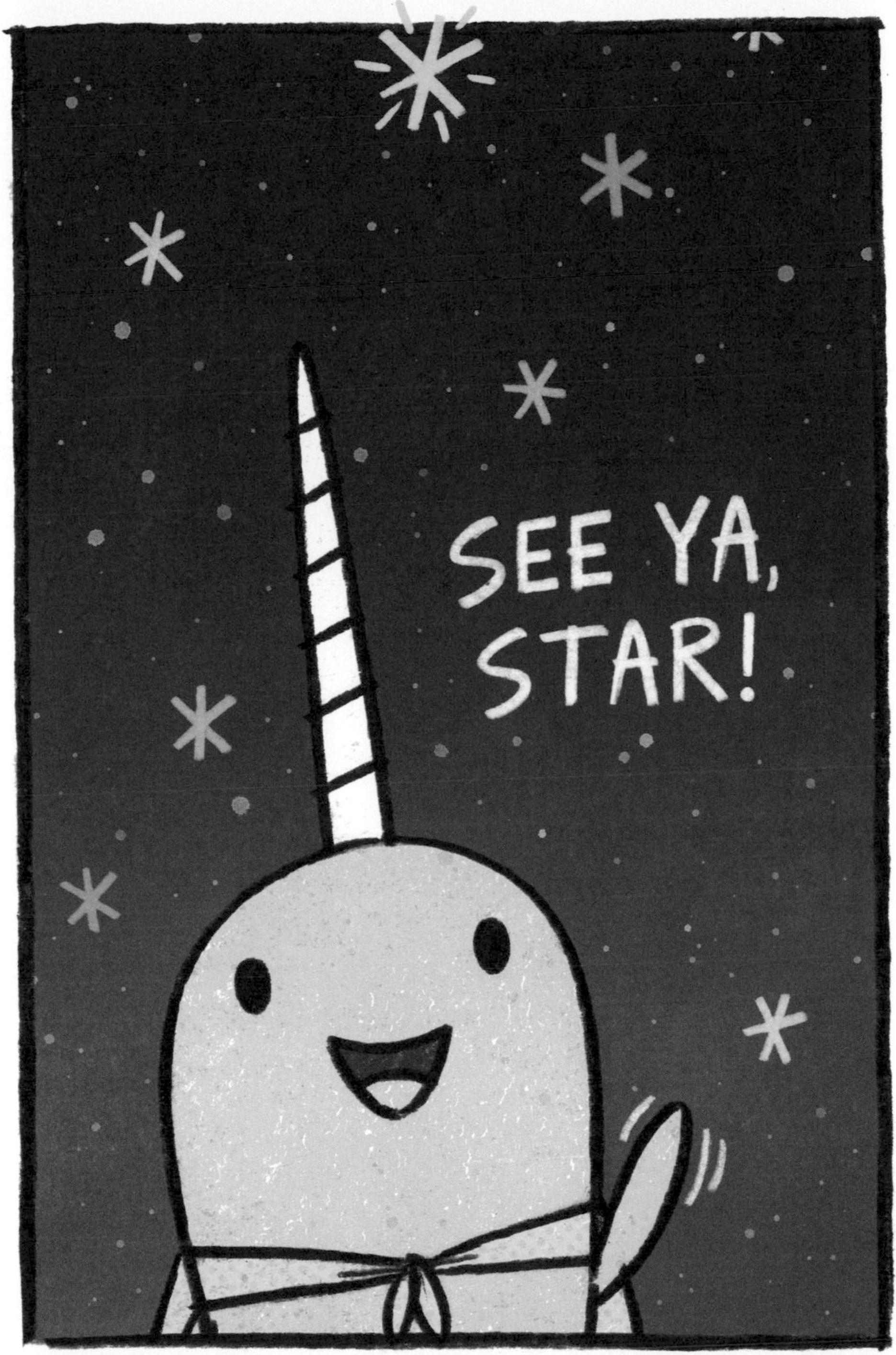
SEE YA,
STAR!

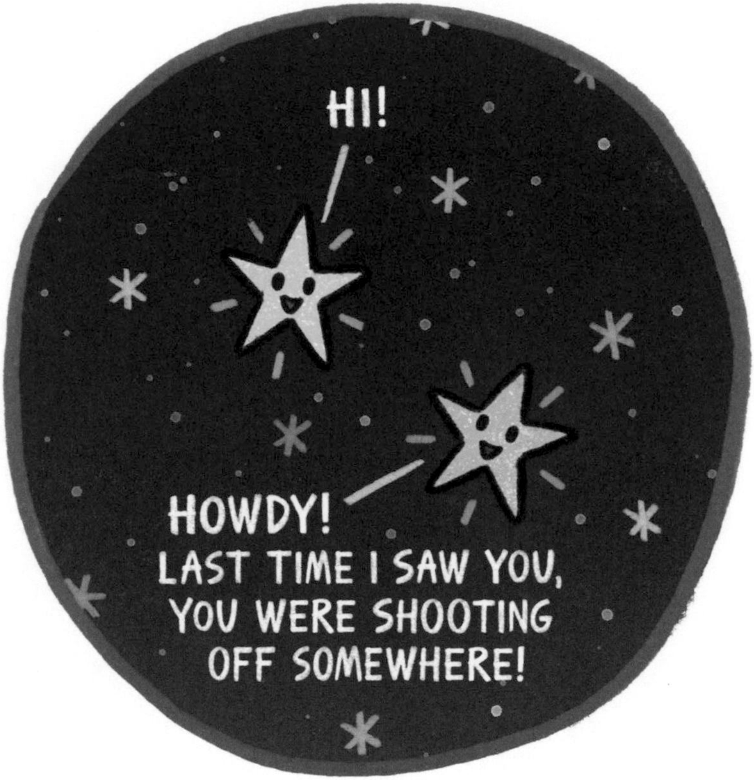
HI!
HOWDY!
LAST TIME I SAW YOU, YOU WERE SHOOTING OFF SOMEWHERE!

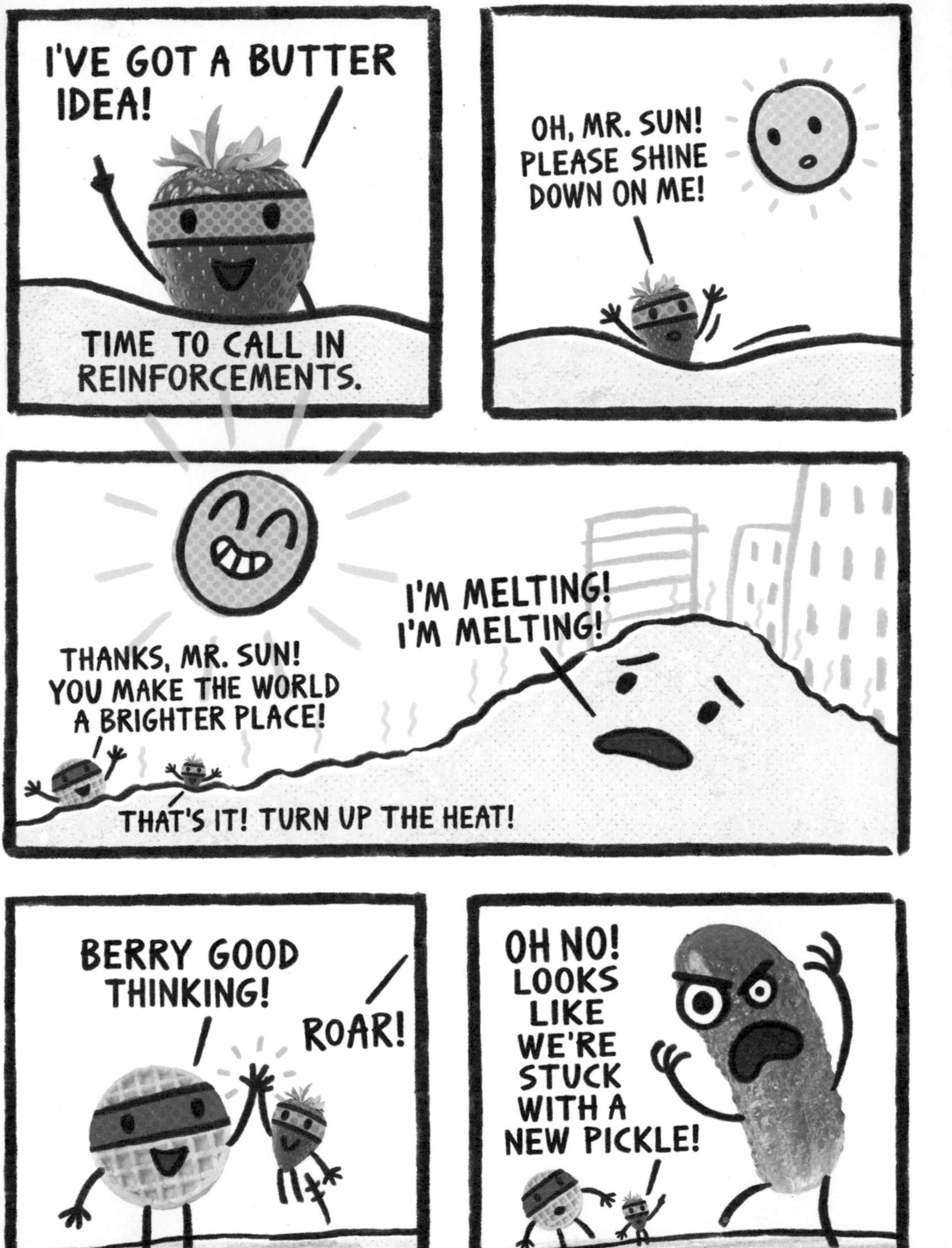
I'VE GOT A BUTTER IDEA!
TIME TO CALL IN REINFORCEMENTS.
OH, MR. SUN! PLEASE SHINE DOWN ON ME!
THANKS, MR. SUN! YOU MAKE THE WORLD A BRIGHTER PLACE!
I'M MELTING! I'M MELTING!
THAT'S IT! TURN UP THE HEAT!
BERRY GOOD THINKING!
ROAR!
OH NO! LOOKS LIKE WE'RE STUCK WITH A NEW PICKLE!

SUPER NARWHAL VS. BLUE JELLY

A.K.A.

THE SUPER SUPERPOWER!

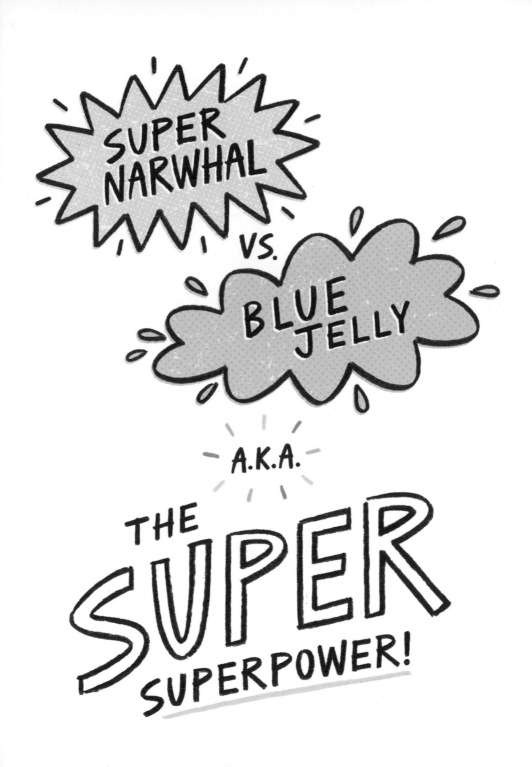

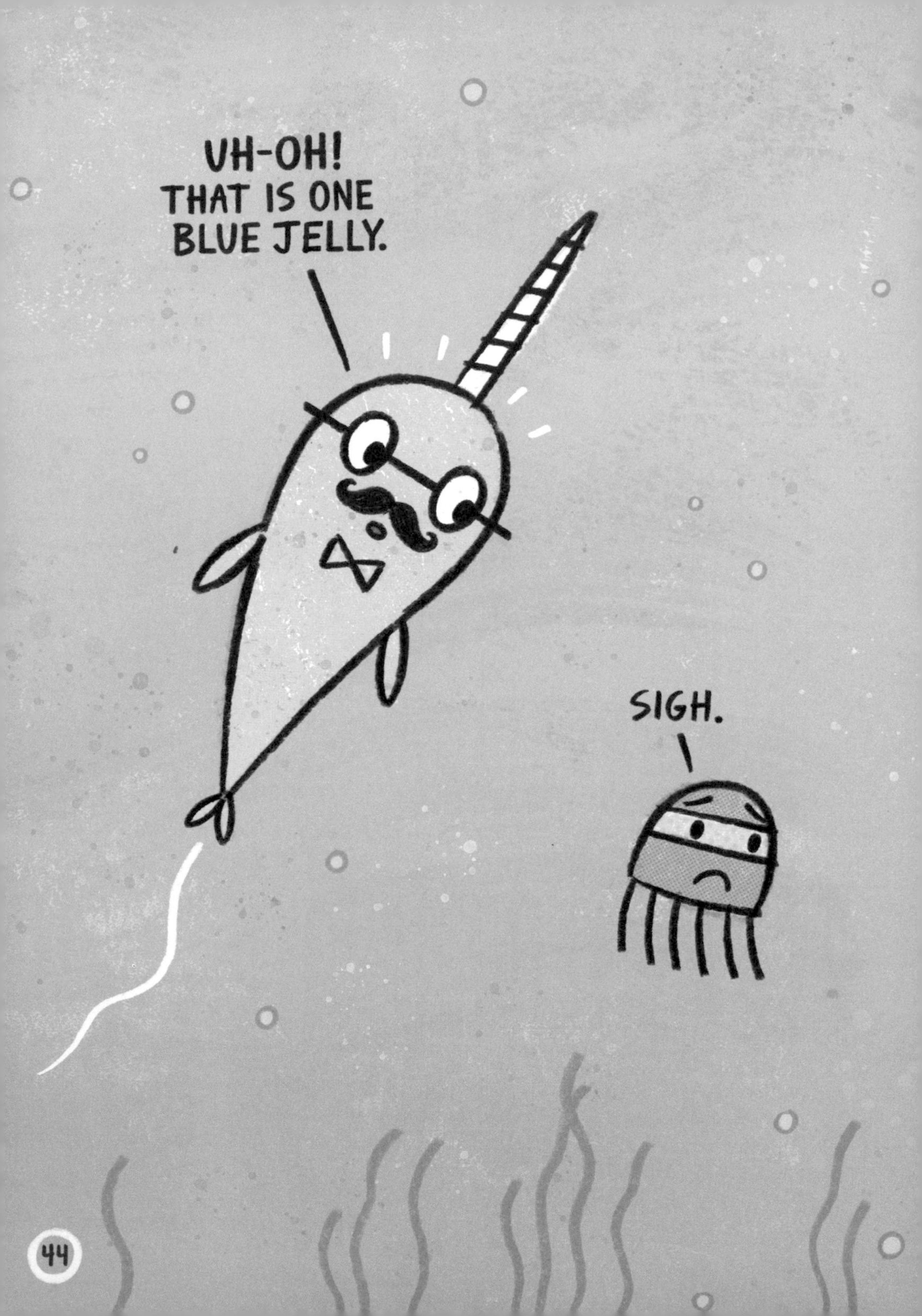
UH-OH!
THAT IS ONE
BLUE JELLY.
SIGH.

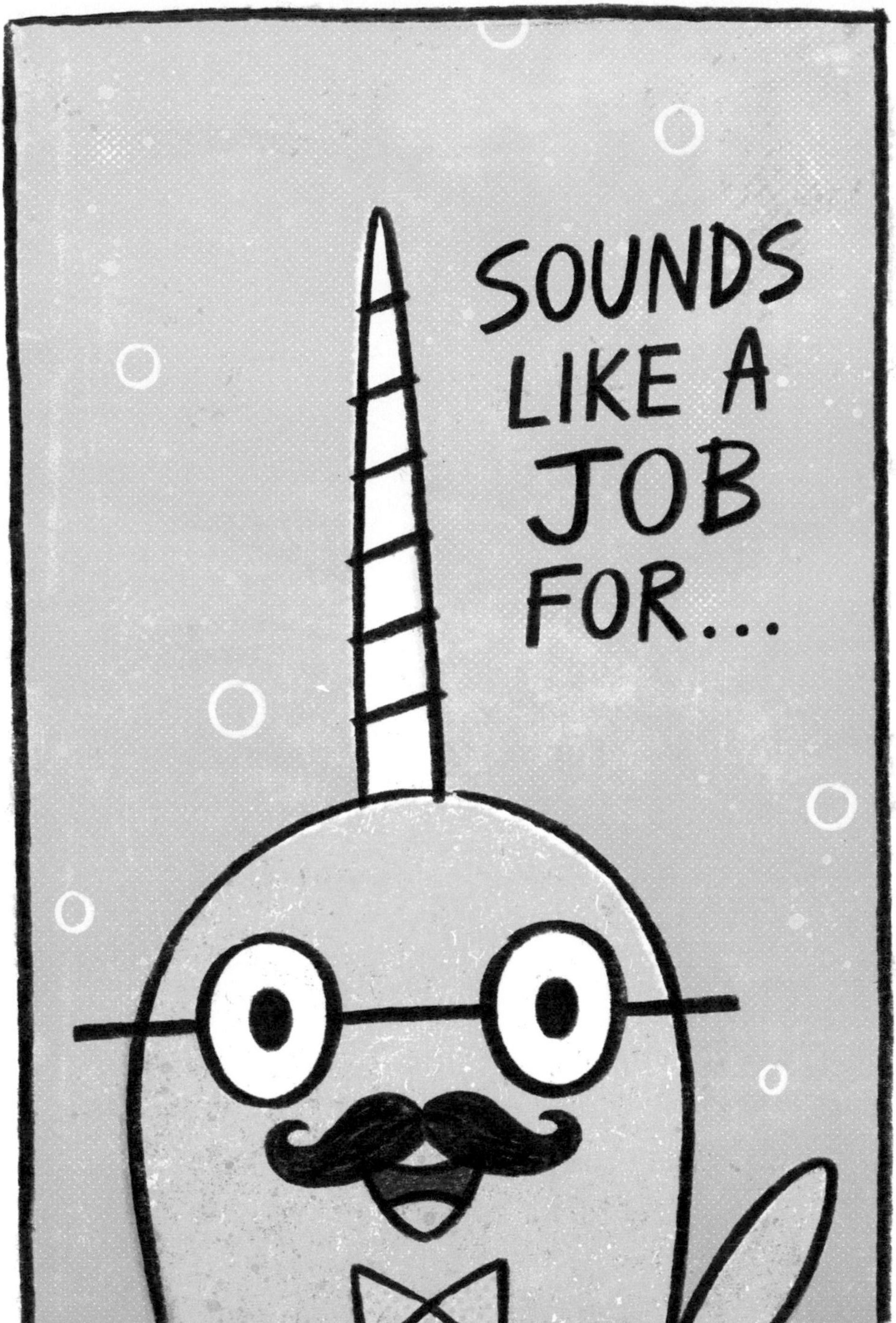
SOUNDS LIKE A JOB FOR...

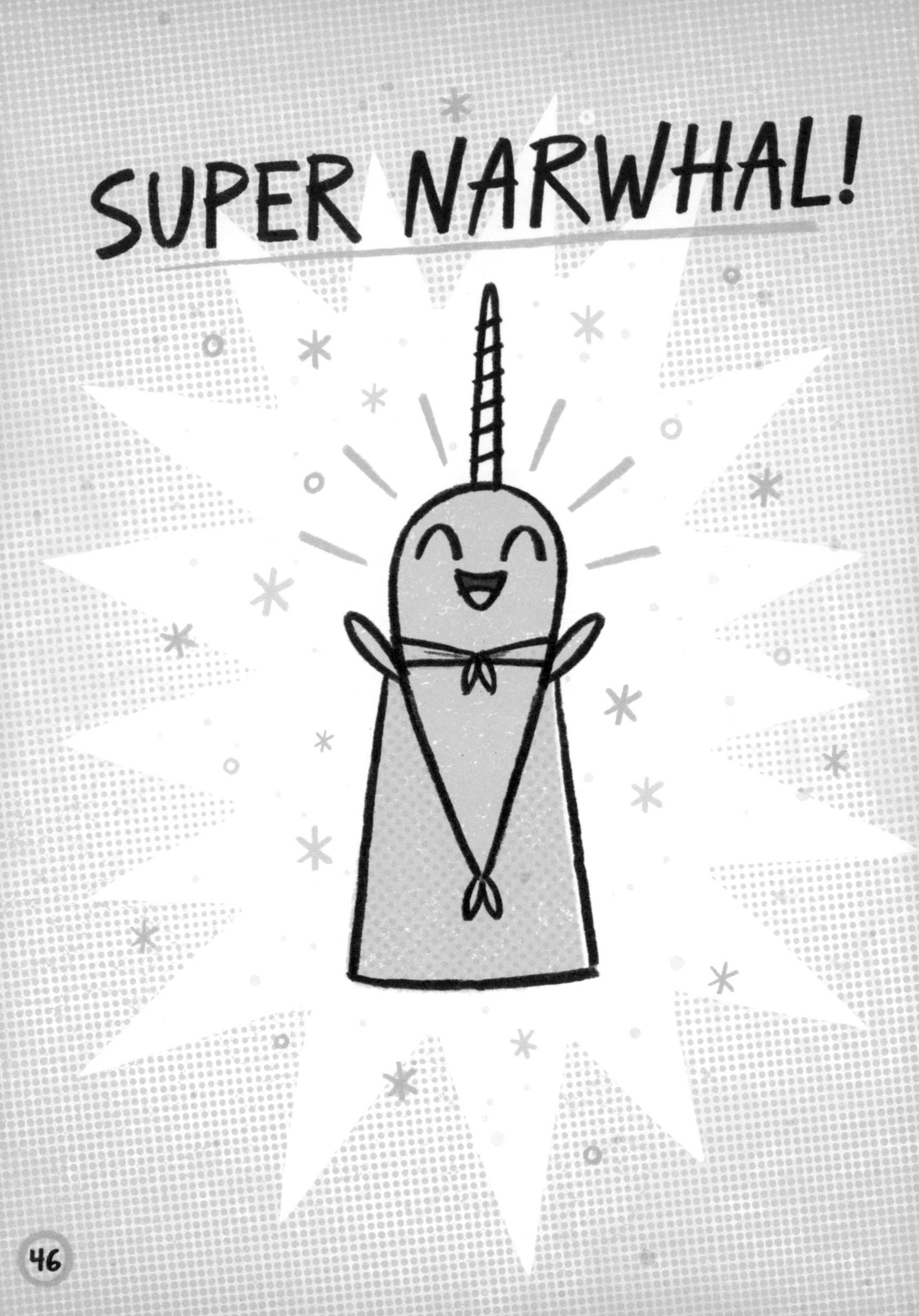
SUPER NARWHAL!

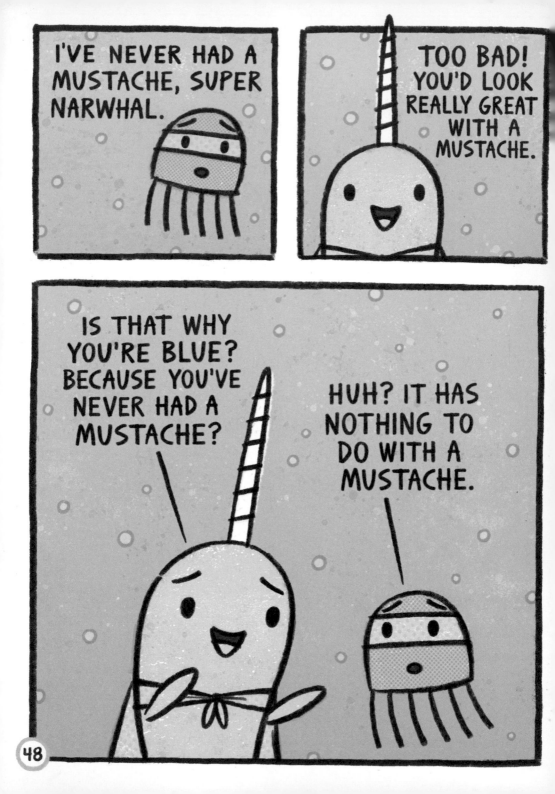

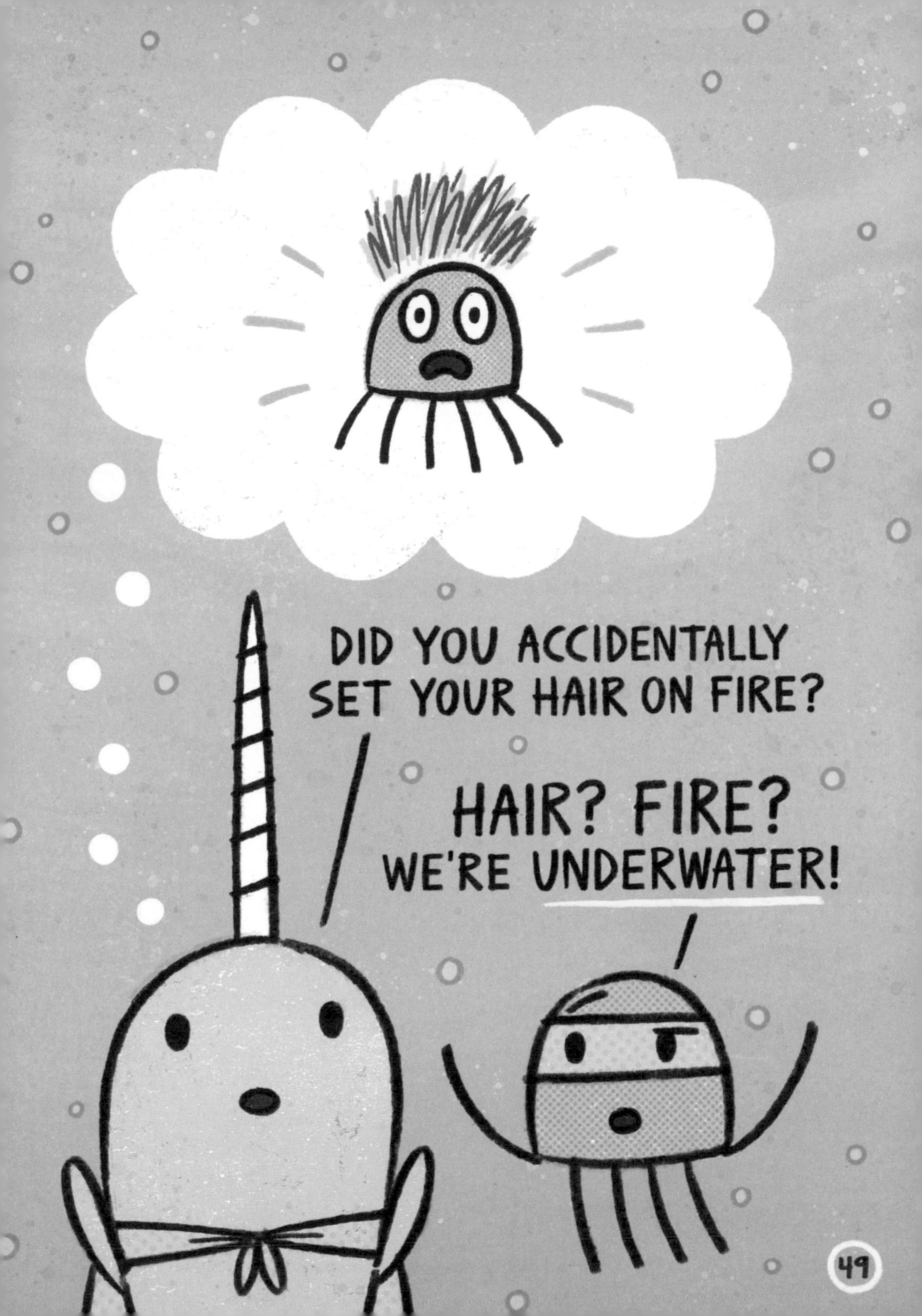
DID YOU ACCIDENTALLY SET YOUR HAIR ON FIRE?
HAIR? FIRE? WE'RE UNDERWATER!

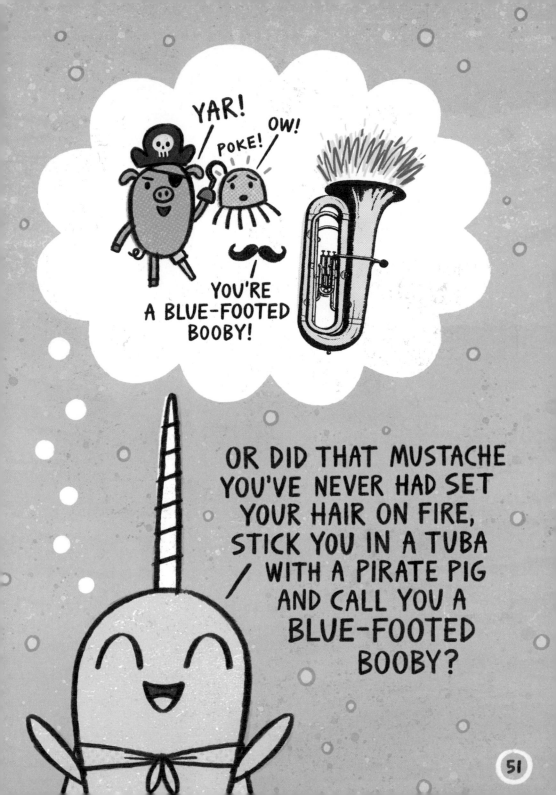

53

OH, WAIT, NOW I REMEMBER...

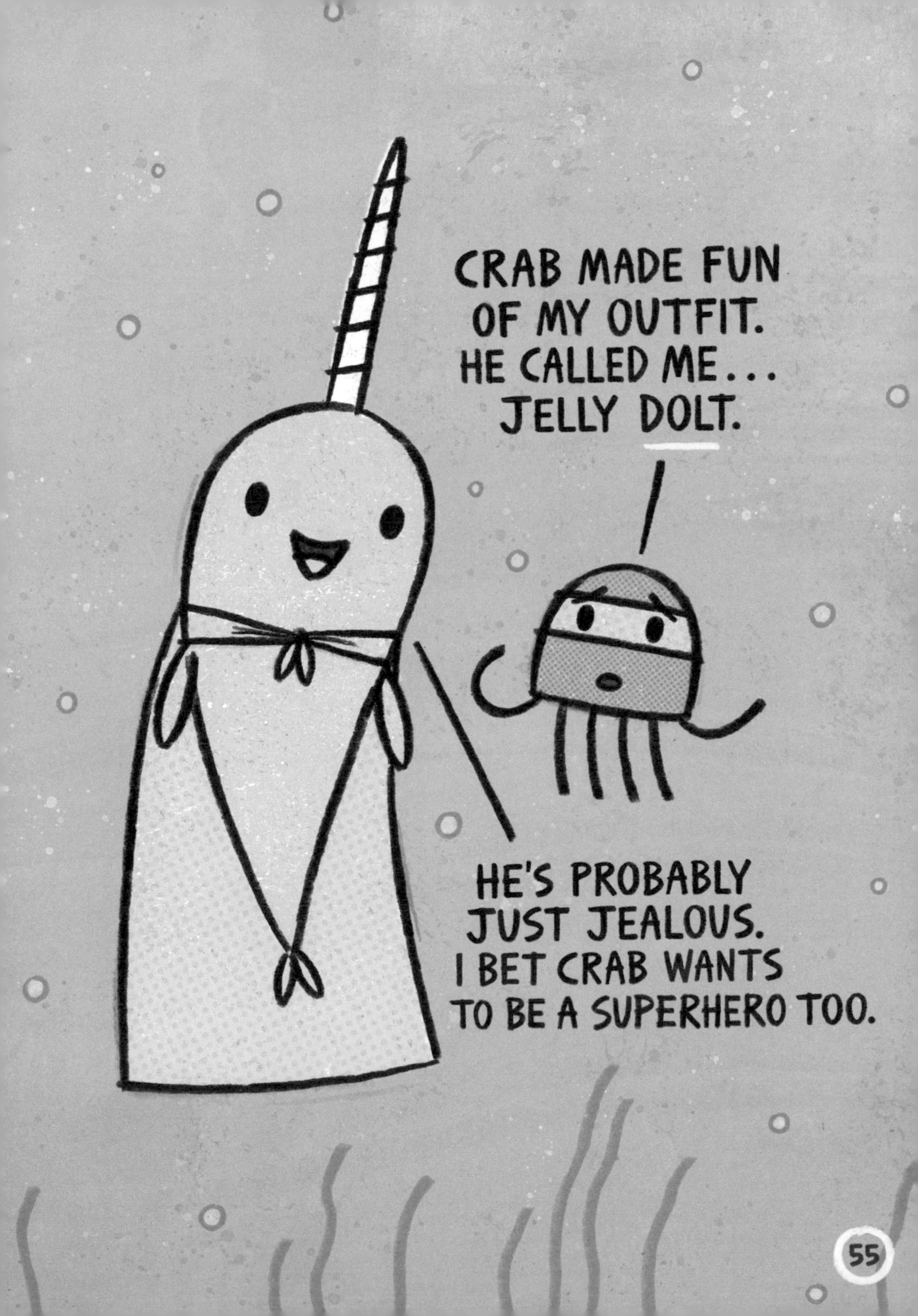
CRAB MADE FUN OF MY OUTFIT. HE CALLED ME... JELLY DOLT.
HE'S PROBABLY JUST JEALOUS. I BET CRAB WANTS TO BE A SUPERHERO TOO.

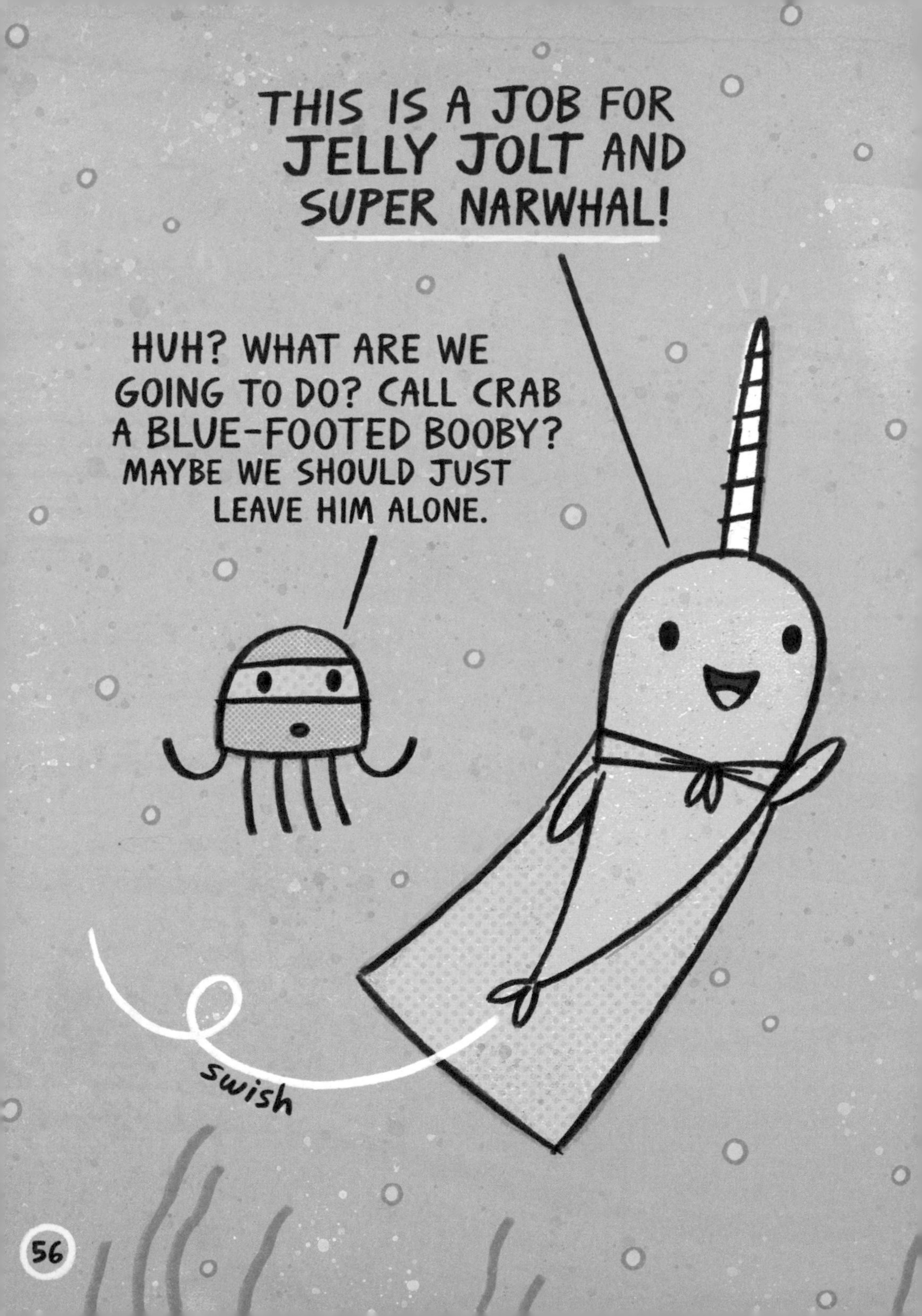
THIS IS A JOB FOR JELLY JOLT AND SUPER NARWHAL!
HUH? WHAT ARE WE GOING TO DO? CALL CRAB A BLUE-FOOTED BOOBY? MAYBE WE SHOULD JUST LEAVE HIM ALONE.
swish

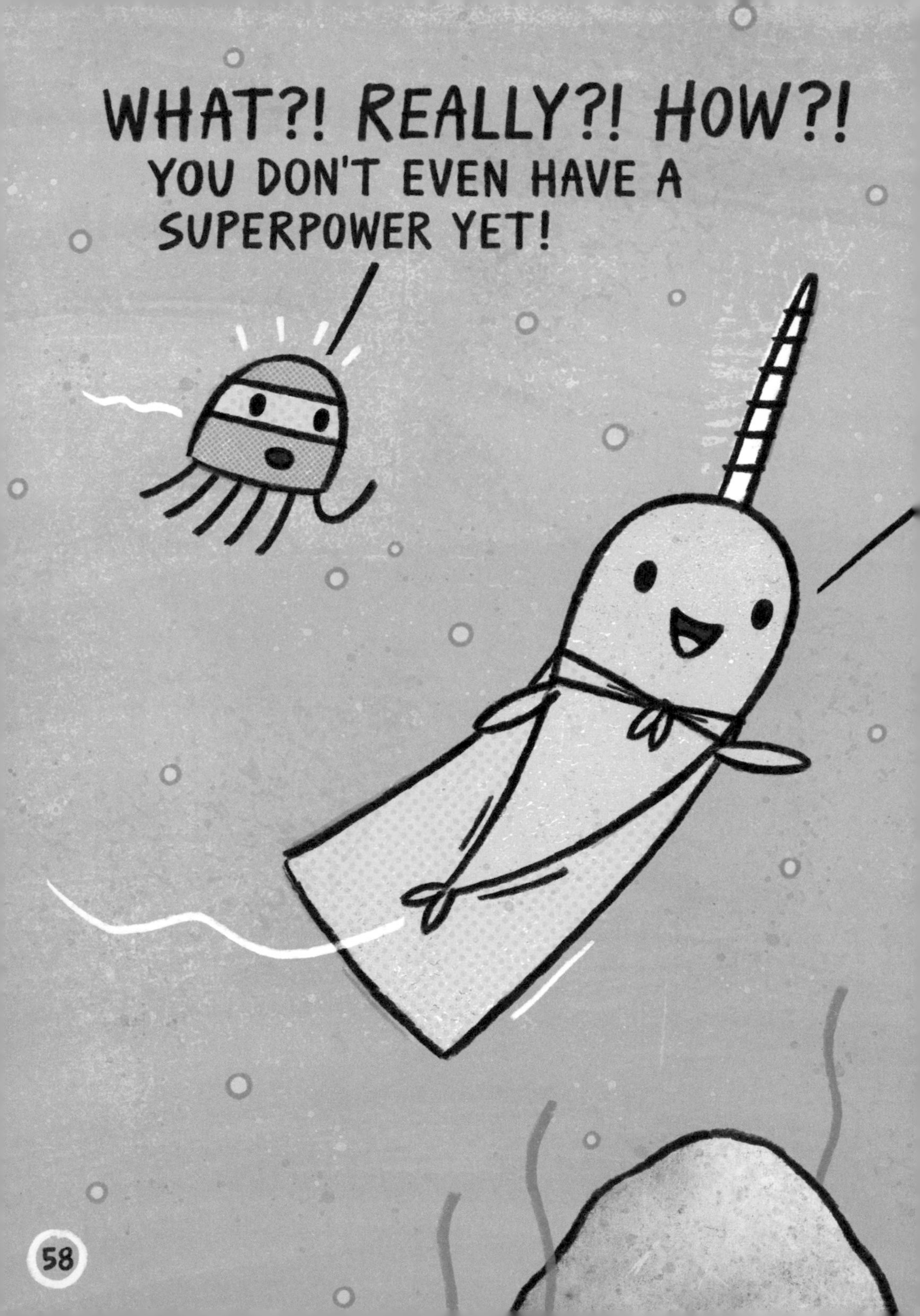
WHAT?! REALLY?! HOW?!
YOU DON'T EVEN HAVE A SUPERPOWER YET!

AHOY, CRAB!
PREPARE TO BE SUPER-FIED!
HUH? SUPER FRIED? BEAT IT, JELLY DOLT! SCRAM, SUPER WHATEVER. I DON'T HAVE TIME FOR YOUR NONSENSE.

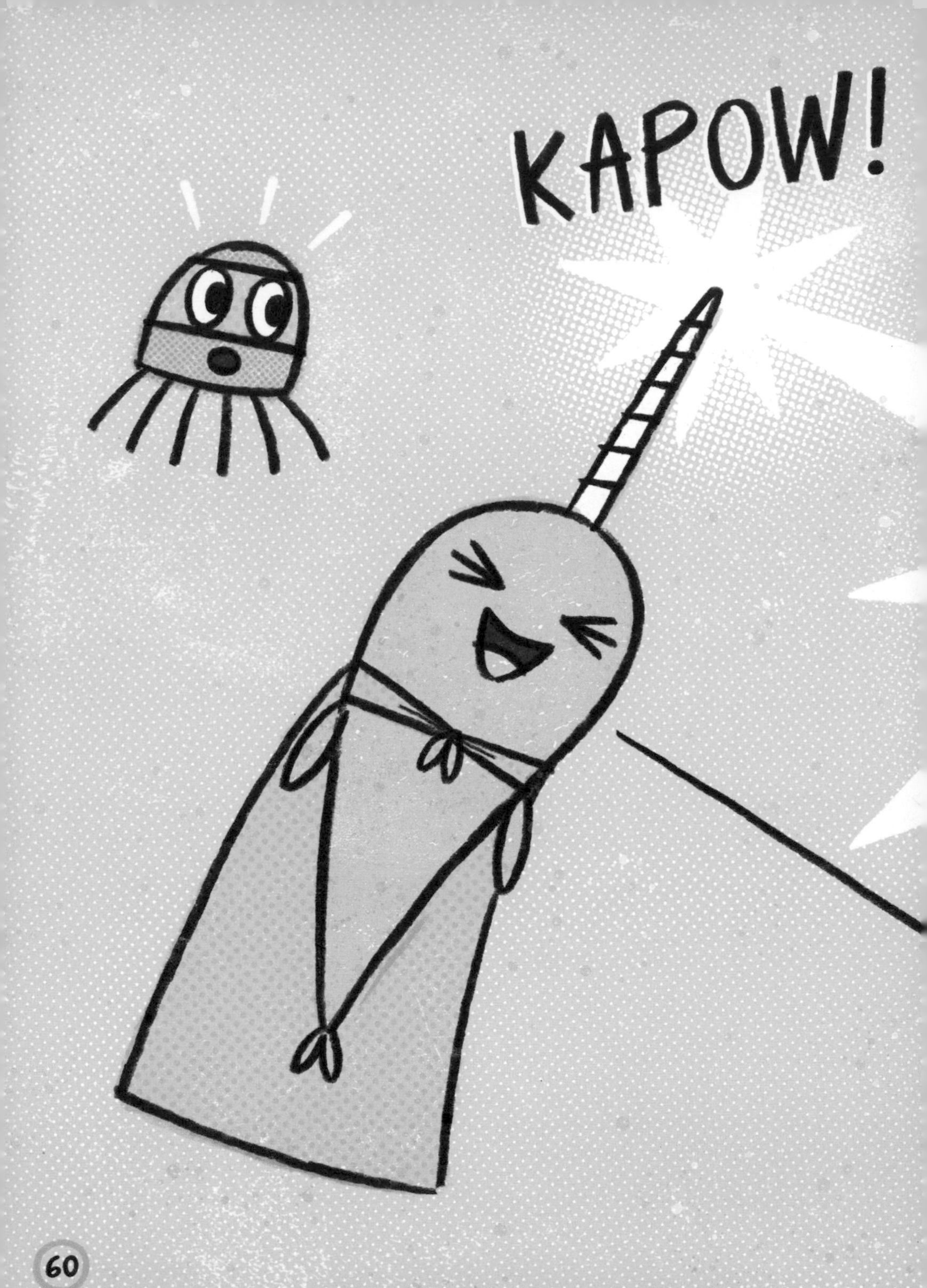
KAPOW!

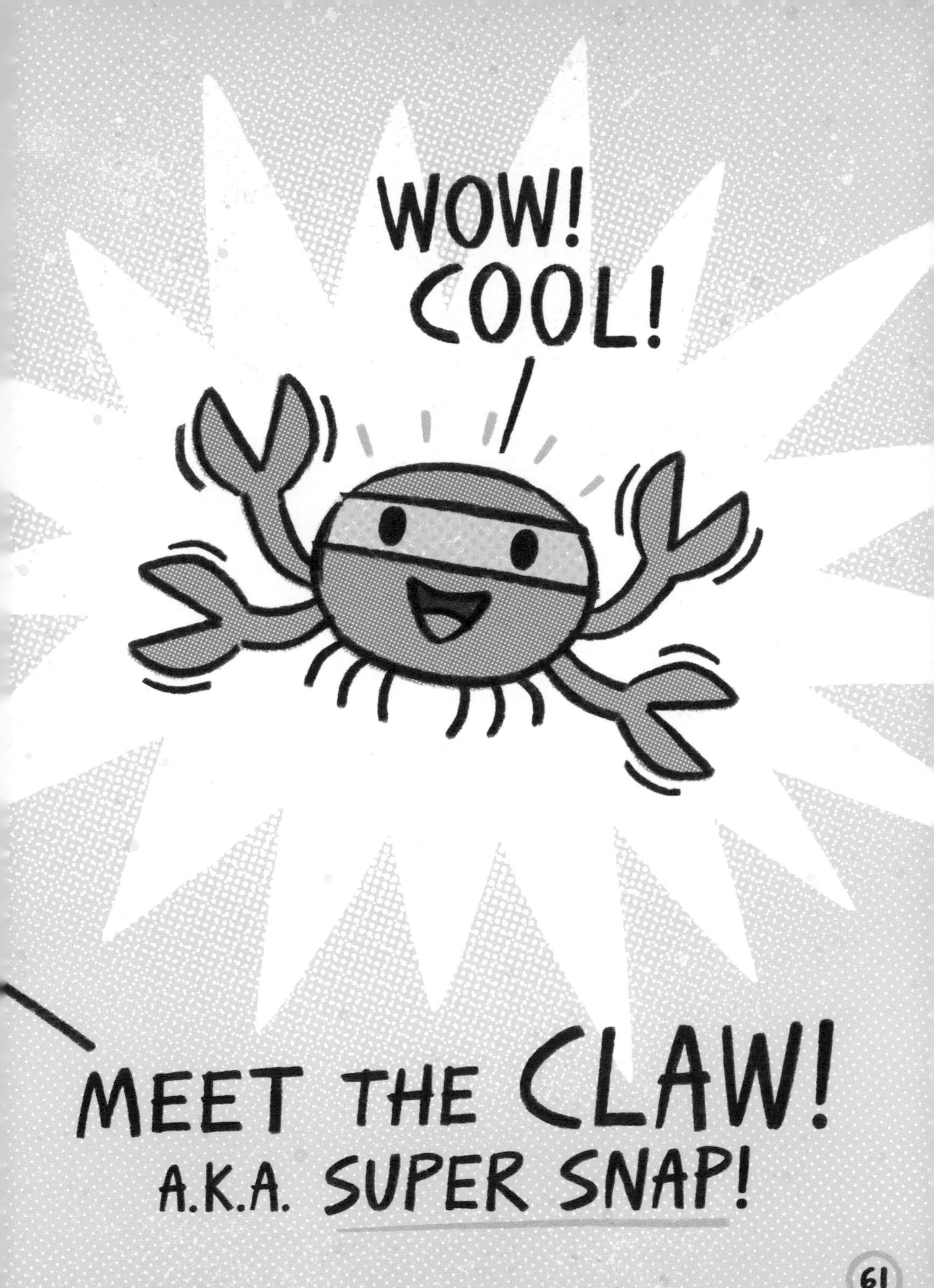
WOW! COOL!
MEET THE CLAW!
A.K.A. SUPER SNAP!

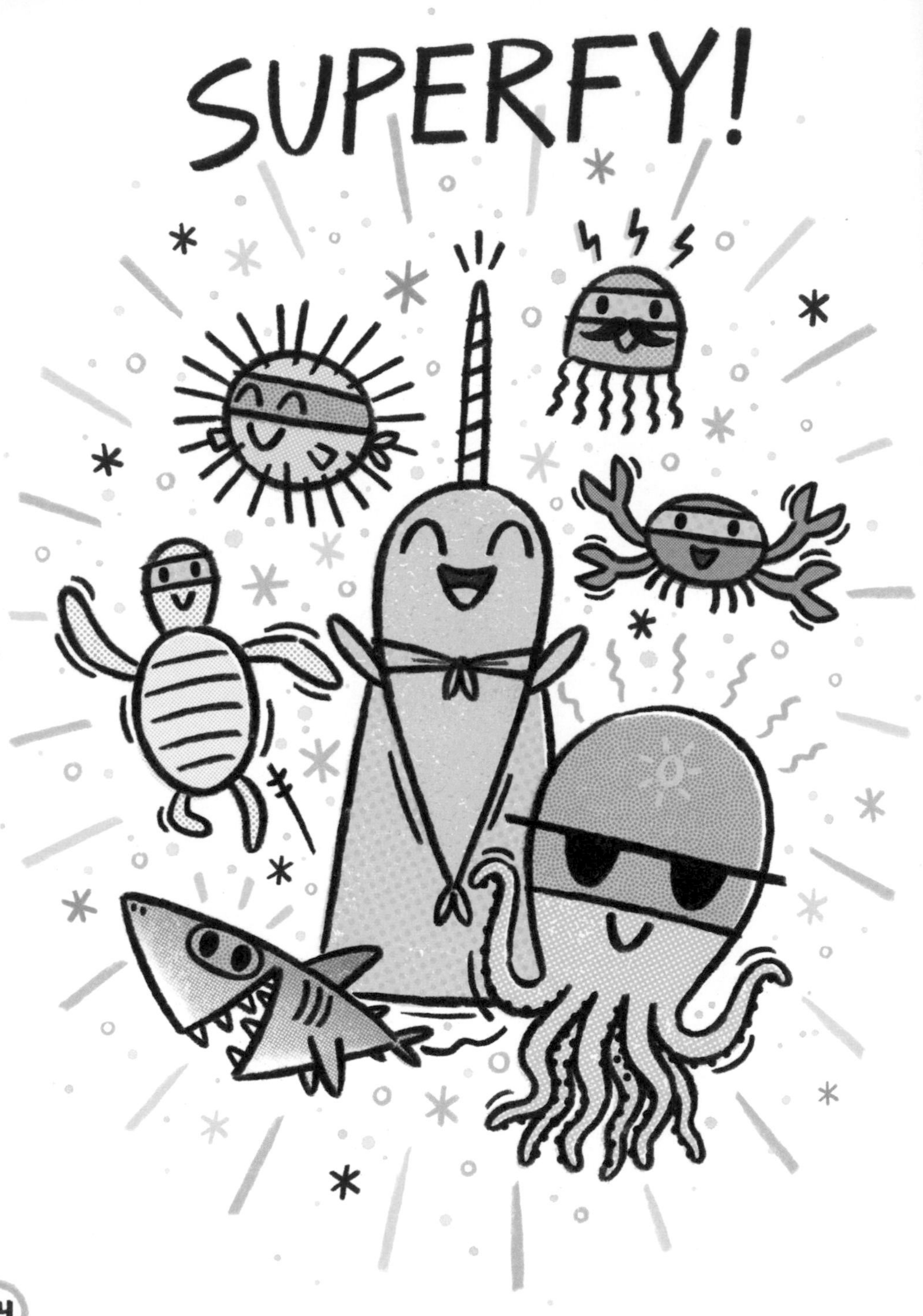
SUPERFY!

MORE NARWHAL AND JELLY ADVENTURES COMING SOON!